The Revolution of Cool

The Revolution of Cool

Kate Breding

iUniverse, Inc.
New York   Bloomington

The Revolution of Cool

Cover art by Emily Young

The views expressed in this work are solely those of the author and do not necessarily reflect the views of the publisher, and the publisher hereby disclaims any responsibility for them.

iUniverse books may be ordered through booksellers or by contacting:

iUniverse
1663 Liberty Drive
Bloomington, IN 47403
www.iuniverse.com
1-800-Authors (1-800-288-4677)

Because of the dynamic nature of the Internet, any Web addresses or links contained in this book may have changed since publication and may no longer be valid.

ISBN: 978-1-4401-8811-4 (sc)
ISBN: 978-1-4502-0803-1 (dj)
ISBN: 978-1-4401-8813-8 (ebk)

Printed in the United States of America

iUniverse rev. date: 01/29/2010

This Book is dedicated to:

My lovely and crazy cousin, KatieRose Pfeffer all my
editors: John and Sarah Breding, Carol L. Brooks, and
Emily Young (another one of my lovely and crazy cousins)

and to my biggest fan: Eddie Breding

Falling into a Hole

✦

Collin

A clean white shirt. No, a clean white T-shirt. Yes, that sounds better. Who would make fun of a clean white T-shirt? Probably Andy Koller. Yes, Andy Koller would definitely make fun of a clean white T-shirt.

But why? Would Andy make fun of a clean black T-shirt? Or a dirty white T-shirt? Yes, Andy would. Because Andy makes fun of everything Collin does. Even if Collin gets an A+ on a math test, Andy would make fun of it.

Collin decided that no matter what he wore, a clean white T-shirt was probably the best choice. But he had to be careful not to get his T-shirt dirty. A dirty T-shirt was bad news. It made him look like a slob, and Collin was absolutely not a slob! Slobs would grow up and be very unsuccessful. But someone like Collin, who wasn't a slob, would grow up and become very successful.

Collin always combed his hair and parted it in the middle, and never wore open toed shoes or left the house without wearing a belt or having his reading glasses safely tucked in his shirt pocket. He didn't wear glasses all the time, just for reading. His best friend Mitch wore glasses all the time because he was near -sighted, and was sort of a slob. He sometimes walked around with his shirt untucked, and that was very slob like in Collin's mind. But for some reason everyone liked slobs.

Andy Koller was a slob, and everyone liked him. He didn't pay attention in class and got a C on almost all his tests, at best. Andy was the sort of person Collin would pass begging on the street in 20 years, while Collin was too busy being successful to notice. Andy never tucked in his shirt, or wore a belt, and never parted his hair, yet he was loved by all. Even Reba! Collin and Reba used to be best friends when they were babies. Reba probably didn't even remember.

Back when they were tiny babies, they would go to Collin's house and run around the house screaming. Everyday they would drive their nanny up the wall. They did everything together: sleep, eat, talk, breath, walk, laugh, get in trouble. Everything. When Reba had to go, she would kick and scream, and so would Collin. They were best friends all the way to kindergarten.

On the first day of kindergarten, they had been scared out of their minds. They had walked into the classroom, side-by-side, and sat down next to each other. Reba had been crying, but since Collin was trying to be a big boy for his dad, Collin only cried a little. And the two kids had hugged each other, as Collin remembered, at the end of the day. Yes, kindergarten had been the best time of Collin's life. Back then, nobody cared about grades, or   shoes, or hair, or level of popularity. Nobody cared the slightest bit. But then in 1st grade, Reba stopped coming to Collin's house as much, and talked to him less and less. By 4th grade she acted as if she never knew him. It was at that same time that everything started mattering.

It was in 4th grade that Andy started teasing Collin and calling him a dork. It was when everyone fell into their groups. It was when Collin was labeled a dork, a geek, a nerd, a loser. It was when Andy had become popular. It was then that Collin fell into a hole that he was sure that no matter how hard he tried, he could never, ever climb out of.

Reba's Secret:

✦

Reba

"Reba is short for Rebecca," Peyton said slowly.

"Alright, what's that got to do with anything?" Reba asked.

"I can call you Rebecca!" Peyton said turning away from the computer screen.

"What? No you can't!" Reba said, alarmed.

"Yes I can! Your real name is Rebecca! Besides, Rebecca is prettier than Reba by a long shot! Reba reminds me of rehab!" Peyton said, twisting a curly strand of golden brown hair around her toasty tan finger.

"Hey! Do I remind you of rehab? Because since you didn't even say 'no offence', I take great offence!" Reba said defensively.

Peyton could act so stuck up sometimes. She could act as if she could say anything and no one would care.

"You don't remind me of rehab Reba, its not you, just your name. So that's why I think I should call you Rebecca from now on," Peyton said matter-of-factly, even though it wasn't a matter of fact.

"My real name is Reba! Go check my birth certificate and see for yourself!" Reba was sure her name was Reba, and not Rebecca.

"I don't need to, because I got the next best thing," Peyton said and then yelled, "MRS. SHYNER!"

Reba's mom came up the staircase holding a dust pan in one hand and a broom in the other.

"Yes girls?" Mrs. Shyner asked.

"Is Reba's real name Rebecca or Reba?" Peyton asked in her innocent voice that made adults love her.

"Reba of course!" Mrs. Shyner said before turning to go back down the stairs.

"Ha!" Reba said poking Peyton.

"Humph! You should still change your name to Rebecca," Peyton said sourly.

"No, I like my name the way it is," Reba said. She couldn't believe she was having this conversation. But, someone like Peyton was used to always getting her way and what she wanted and being right because she was a spoiled, only child. Not that all only children were spoiled. Reba's cousin Nicole was an only child, and she wasn't the least bit stuck up or spoiled with unnecessary luxuries.

"Reba, what do you wanna do?" Peyton whined.

"I don't know. What do you wanna do?" Reba asked.

"Uhm, let's play a trick on Collin! He lives up the street from you, doesn't he?" Peyton asked, looking excited.

"Nah," Reba said. Collin didn't need to be humiliated any more than when he was at school.

"Ah c'mon! Pleeeese!" Peyton begged, "Don't be such a goody-good!"

"Fine, but nothing too bad okay?" Reba sighed.

"Yes! Don't worry Reba you won't get caught! I promise!" Peyton said. But before they could start to plot what to do to Collin, Peyton's mom honked outside.

"Bye," Peyton said as she skipped to her car.

Reba sighed as she watched Peyton leave. Peyton was the sort of friend that you had to be very outgoing to get along with. Reba wasn't outgoing, but somehow Peyton ended up on Reba's top five best friends list. Reba was fine with it though. As long as she had other friends besides Peyton to hang out with, she was perfectly all right.

But just to make sure, Reba dived under her bed and took out her top five best friends list. Yes, there they were. The wonderful names that she was glad to say were her best friends' names: Abigail, Kat, Brooke, Erin and Peyton. Good, all there. Her worst nightmare was to not have any friends at all. This had happened before, and Reba had barely got by 4th grade with the friends she had. At that time they hadn't even called her their friends, just some annoying girl that tagged along with them. But now she had friends; she even had best friends, this was good. And she could tell these friends anything, anything at all, because they were her friends. Wait, almost everything. She could tell her friends almost everything.

There was one secret that Reba had never told anyone, and never would. She had gone to all costs to keep this secret secret. This secret was; Reba was deaf. Only in one ear though, not both ears. She was going to get surgery when she was five, but her mother had said that as long as Reba could still hear, the surgery would be a waste of money. Her mother had also turned down a hearing aid, using the same excuse. At the time, Reba had been disappointed. She wanted something that people would oh and ah over. Something that would make her stand out. But now Reba couldn't be more thankful with her mother's choice. It would be so embarrassing, a living nightmare, if she had a hearing aid at the age 13! She was so glad that nobody knew. Suddenly Reba sat up straight. Someone did know: Collin.

The Revolution of Cool:

✦

Collin

"Stop it!" Collin cried as Andy taunted him by threatening to break his glasses.

"Uh uh uh!" Andy said and then threw them to Reese who caught them with ease.

"C'mon you guys!" Collin begged. If these glasses broke, he probably wouldn't be able to read for a week!

"No way man!" Reese said throwing the glasses high above his head, and catching them just one foot before they hit the ground.

Just then, the new kid, Cole, who had been hanging out with Andy, walked in.

"'Sup guys? Oh," Cole observed the scene.

"Catch!" Reese tossed Cole the glasses.

"Whose are these?" Cole asked.

"Mine!" Collin shrieked.

"Yah! Throw 'em here!" Andy said waving his arms.

"Is this your guy's idea of fun? I think we have better things to do than pick on this kid," Cole said looking bored, before tossing

Collin his glasses and leaving. Collin smiled at his hero and then held onto his glasses tight before leaving as fast as he could.

Around the corner he ran into Mitch and Steve. Steve was holding his electronic encyclopedia and pointing at it with much over exaggerated movement.

"See! See! Look! Look!" Steve said, making his mad face. Steve's face was red and his eyes were huge. His lower lip trembled and his upper one was stuck out.

"Gee! Hey Collin!" Mitch ran over to Collin and slapped him on the back.

"Hey guys," Collin said nodding to Steve and Mitch.

"Collin, I'm trying to tell Mitch that Daddy Long Legs are poisonous!" Steve said.

"Uh, I don't really know that," Collin said, "But you guys, you'll never guess what just happened! Andy and Reese took my glasses and then the new guy came in and made them stop!"

"I never liked that new guy. If he is Andy's friend, he is an enemy of mine!" Steve said defiantly.

"No! He *stopped* them from teasing me!" Collin explained.

"Oh, hum," Steve pondered this for a while.

"Hey! Today is a new day! If he stuck up for you, then imagine what else he might do! We could be on the top of the popularity list!" Mitch said, punching his fist in the air.

"Mitch, please tuck in your shirt! You are being so slob like!" Collin said, rolling his eyes. Mitch could have some pretty crazy ideas sometimes, but this idea was nice to think about. If Collin was at the top of the list, and then he could change the concepts of cool! Reba might talk to him again, and he could wear a clean white T-shirt without stopping to think of how much he would be teased.

"No way! If today I become head of the list, I wanna do it coolly!" Mitch said, puffing out his chest.

"But that's it! We will be the new revolution of cool! So what ever we do will be cool! You don't want coolness to be slobness do you?" Collin asked.

"No, but having your shirt untucked isn't slob like," Mitch said defensively.

"It is in my book!" Collin said and then the bell rang and the three of them went to class.

During lunch, Mitch, Steve, Collin, Robert, and Antonio walked the track together.

"I still think that the revolution is right around the corner!" Mitch said, jabbing Collin in the ribs with his elbow.

"What do you keep talking about with this 'revolution'?" Robert questioned.

"Mitch thinks that the new kid, Cole, is going to get us to the top of the list, and then we will be the role models of cool," Collin explained.

"What is this list?" Antonio asked.

"The list of social ranks," Steve said smartly.

"The list of popularity," Collin explained again.

"Where are we on that list?" Robert asked.

"Uh, right now, the bottom," Mitch said sadly.

"And you think that in one day we will be at the top?" Robert asked amazed.

"Maybe," Mitch said, shrugging.

"Ah, what it would be like. I could teach people to respect people of Latino origin! No more will we be mistaken for Mexicans-" Antonio said fiercely.

"But Antonio, you are Mexican," Collin pointed out.

"No! I was born in Mexico, but all my family is Latin! My mom just happened to be in Mexico when she gave birth to me!" Antonio said.

"Oh," Collin said, "Are you sure you aren't Mexican? Because you have a Mexican accent and you look Mexican."

"No no no! I am Latino! Not Mexican!" Antonio said, stomping his foot.

"Dude, you don't even know your background when it is written on your face? Talk about a dork," Andy Koller said from behind them.

"Go away Andy," Steve said, turning red.

"It's a free country," Reese said from next to Andy.

"Yah, but we have a right to our own privacy!" Steve shot at him.

"The country is still free," Reese shot back. Steve looked to Cole for help, but Cole was looking at Andy. Now that Collin saw Cole up close, there was something familiar about Cole's ice blue eyes and sandy hair, like a forgotten memory that couldn't be retrieved.

"Besides, what could you guys be talking about that you wouldn't want us to hear?" Andy asked, falling into stride with Steve.

"Yah? What?" Reese asked as he walked backwards in front of them, pulling Cole along with him.

"Nothing you need to know about! We just don't want to talk with you guys that's all!" Steve said defensively.

"Ooo! Dis!" Reese crooned.

"What wouldn't you want us to know about? We have the right to knowing stuff. We want to know this," Andy said, putting his arm around Steve.

"We have a right to privacy," Steve tried to say as he attempted to get Andy's arm off his shoulder.

"Just tell us! Don't be a wimp!" Reese jeered.

"Steve isn't a wimp!" Robert said defensively.

"Then why won't he tell us what he doesn't want to tell us?" Reese said, sticking his face in Robert's.

"Because he doesn't want to! Now go away!" Robert said.

"We don't want to!" Andy announced tightening his grip on Steve's shoulder.

"This is so boring! Isn't there anything else you guys do for fun?" Cole said to Andy and Reese.

Andy looked at Cole respectfully.

"Well yah, I guess there is," Andy said, letting go of Steve and looking ashamed that he let Cole down.

The three boys walked away without looking back.

Mitch turned to Steve, Collin, Robert and Antonio.

"What did I tell you?" he grinned.

The Twins:

Reba

Reba came home from school, and it was a normal day. Her friend's still liked her, she still had a mountain of homework , and she still lived in her attic room.

As Reba began on her homework, Marie and Kevin burst in the door followed by Lily. Marie and Lily were Reba's 16 year old twin sisters. Identical twins. And Kevin: Marie's boyfriend that practically lived at Reba's house.

Marie and Lily looked alike, but in a way, they didn't. Unless you were to get extremely descriptive you could find no difference between them. They both had short brown curly hair and soft brown eyes. But in a way you just knew they were different.

Maybe it was the hair. Marie's hair was more bouncy and fresh. Probably because Marie shampooed it so very well and took such good care of it. Lily's hair sort of drooped by her shoulders; the curls weren't as enthusiastic as Maries. They looked fragile, as if one meet with a brush and they would be gone forever. It was hard to say what made them look so different, but yet so much the same.

Maybe because Marie was a girly-girl and wasn't afraid to show it. She wore makeup, and wore the in-style clothing and went shopping practically every other day, and got a manicure once a week. Her face gave off the impression of snottieness. She was, but what older sister-teenager isn't?

Lily on the other hand was a sporty-girl. Her wardrobe consisted of sports jerseys and baggy shorts. She had sort of a glint in her eye that even when she wasn't smiling, made you think she was. She was a little bit of a better sister to Reba then Marie was. Lily helped Reba with her homework, sometimes, and gave her a heads up on how to get on certain teachers' good sides, and gave her tips for getting on sports teams, even though Reba wasn't into that.

And now we come back to where Marie and Kevin burst in the door followed by Lily.

"Hey there little sister!" Marie said ruffling Reba's hair.

"Hi," Reba said.

"Mom wants to know if you want cheese on your hamburger or not?" Marie asked.

"No cheese," Reba said, turning back to her homework.

"No cheese!" Marie shouted down the stairs.

"What ya doing little sis?" Marie asked, sitting on Reba's desk.

"Oh! Mrs. Latorre! Ouch!" Lily said, wincing.

What do you want?" Reba asked. She knew that her sisters would never waste their time to be with her. Maybe Lily, but for sure never Marie.

"Why do we need to want something to hang out with our little sister?" Marie asked in a pout voice. Reba only raised her eyebrows.

"But since you asked," Marie continued, "Could we borrow your hair curler and lip gloss set?"

"Where is yours?" Reba asked.

"That demon dog next door stole my curler, and I am almost out of lip gloss anyway," Marie said, sticking her nose in the air and throwing her hair over her shoulder.

"I wonder why," Reba said under her breath. Marie wore lip gloss so much that few people have seen her without a shiny layer of flavor covering her lips.

"What?" Lily asked.

"I said alright," Reba said loudly. Marie smiled and ran over to the corner of Reba's attic room, grabbed her hair curler and lip gloss bag and ran down stairs, with Kevin and Lily at her heels.

Not Going There Again:

✦

Collin

Collin stared at his plate. He wasn't actually looking at his food, though. He was thinking, thinking about Cole. Why had Cole stuck up for them? And why had Andy not objected? No one ever stuck up for them. Ever. But now Cole did, and Andy didn't do anything about it. He listened to Cole, took orders from Cole, and if Cole stuck up for the unpopular, then Andy would stop teasing them.

"Eat your greenies dear, they are getting cold," Collin's mom said in her Texan drawl.

"Mom, when you were in school, um, where were you on the social rank?" Collin dared to ask.

"Huh," His mother pondered while chewing on a single green bean, "I say I wasn't down with all the loners, that is for sure, but definitely not popular either. I'll say I was normal. I had friends, no one teased me. I was pretty normal."

"Pretty normal," he said, pondering. "Did you have a lot of friends? Did people ever call you and your friends names?" Collin ventured.

"Names, well my friend Patty was sometimes called Patty Cake. That is about it," His mother said, swallowing her green bean. Collin nodded and delivered a cold green bean into his mouth.

The next morning Mitch was really trying his luck. He wore the most nerdish outfit he owned; even Steve thought it was a little too spiffy and corky.

"Why are you wearing that? You know you will only get teased," Collin told him.

"No I won't, watch!" Mitch said and pulled his pants up so high that they went over his belly button. Then he marched over to where Andy and Reese and Cole were standing.

"Hey, looking good Mathews!" Reese jeered.

Andy jumped up and ran past Mitch, and grabbed his glasses off his face.

"Hey! Give those back!" Mitch said. Collin knew that Mitch couldn't see more than about three feet in front of him without his glasses. Andy swiftly tossed them to Reese.

"Looooser!" Reese and Andy chanted at Mitch. Collin fought back the urge to stick up for his friend.

"Are you serious?" Cole asked.

Collin saw Mitch grin slightly.

"Yeah," Andy said quietly.

"C'mon, let's go do something else," Cole said.

Reese looked at Andy; Andy nodded and pushed Mitch's glasses onto his face.

"What did I tell you? We have someone on our side. He is like a secret agent, appearing to work for Evil Andy and Reese, but is actually secretly on our side!" Mitch chuckled.

"Mitch!" Steve said, raising his hands, "You're right!"

Collin smiled with Mitch and Steve as Robert came over to them, and the bell rang.

During lunch Mitch was going to try his luck again but Collin, Steve, Antonio, and Robert told him not to. Mitch was very proud of himself as he made a big show of eating sliced apples, peanut butter and jelly, a juice box, and some whole wheat crackers. Collin watched as Andy laughed at them from his table. Andy sipped at his Diet Coke and munched on his pizza.

"Sugar," Steve said, shaking his head, "No wonder they don't do well in school."

"Your lunch was a very good pick today," Steve told Mitch, "Although that juice could have been water."

"Do you really think food affects how you learn?" Robert asked Steve.

"Of course!" Steve said importantly. Collin didn't listen to the conversation. He was focusing on Cole.

Cole was eating the same lunch as Mitch, except for water instead of a juice box. Collin found this very interesting since Andy and Reese were having a small sugar fest.

"Collin!" Mitch said loudly, "Are you listening to me?"

"Sorry," Collin mumbled.

"This is very important since you are the main part!" Antonio informed.

"Main part?" Collin asked, confused.

"Yes, you have to go up to Cole after school and invite him to hang out with us at lunch, okay?" Mitch said.

"That is a little over the top, don't you think?" Collin asked hopefully.

"No. This experiment is an important one," Steve said sharply.

"Why am I the main part?" Collin asked.

"Because you introduced us to Cole's kind ways," Mitch explained.

Collin nodded and bit into his bologna.

After school Collin rushed to get to Cole. He found Cole walking home across the football field.

"Hey!" Collin yelled.

Cole stopped, not even turning to see who it was.

"Hi," Collin said when he caught up to Cole.

When he saw Collin, he showed no sign of disgust or anything that Collin usually got from Andy. Cole's face showed no emotion of being around Collin.

"I wanted to thank you that day when you stuck up for me," Collin said sheepishly.

Cole shrugged.

"And wanted to invite you to sit and eat lunch with us tomorrow," Collin invited.

"You mean like hang out?" Cole asked, turning to face Collin.

"Yes!" Collin said hopefully.

"No way! I'm not going there again!" Cole said before quickening his pace to a run and leaving Collin more curious than ever.

"Not going there *again*?" Mitch repeated the next morning when Collin told him.

"Yes," Collin sighed.

"Does he mean bottom of the social rank again, or what?" Mitch asked.

"I don't know. Steve might though," Collin offered.

"Know what?" Steve asked as he approached. Mitch and Collin quickly explained what had happened.

"Well, lets see, maybe he was at the bottom of the social rank before?" Steve suggested.

"That's what we thought too," Collin commented.

"Well, there is only one way to find out; ask him," Steve said plainly.

Rumor of the Nerd Protector:

♦

Reba

It is extremely hard to act like you are doing something when there is nothing to do. That was Reba's case. Coach Fortman had decided that instead of playing soccer during PE that they should play football. Flag football. Some of the boys had groaned when they heard this, but Reba felt only 1% better. Flag football and football were still football; a dangerous sport that required catching, and throwing, two things that Reba could not do for her life.

But the boys were really excited about playing flag football, even without the tackling, so Reba hoped that there would be enough boys so that the ball would not have to be thrown to her. Reba hoped she could stand in the background and act like she was in the game. Maybe one of her friends would be on her team with her, and she could stand and talk to her in the background. Only Kat was in Reba's PE class. The rest of her friends had PE in a different period.

Reba looked over to Kat as Coach Fortman picked the teams. Kat's eyes were big and at the same time bored. Reba looked back to Coach.

"And number 17!" Coach yelled.

That was Reba. Reba sighed and looked at Kat, who was looking back at her and raised her eyebrows as if to say, "Too bad, maybe next time".

"And this team will be team B. You will play against A on the middle field. As soon as you have your flags on you can start playing," Coach said, pointing all over.

Reba put on her flags and followed her team to the middle field. There were only three boys and four girls, Reba observed. She hoped that the boys would cover for the girls or that some of the other girls would want to play. But Reba would be okay, she knew, as long as she acted like she was doing something.

This was hard though, because Reba had trouble following what was going on. Why was her team moving to the other side of the field when they just kicked? Who is kicking again? There wouldn't be anything to do anyway even if Reba had any idea of what was going on. The boys were doing a good enough job of playing the game.

Coach walked over to watch team B (Reba's team) play against team A. Only one girl was actually in the game. But not much, she was basically running a little to follow when the boys (they were the only ones playing) ran, but not fast enough to be open to catch, just enough to look like she was playing. The rest of the girls on team B were standing around, picking their nails and talking to their friends. As Reba's team began to walk over to the other side of the field again for some reason that Reba didn't know.

Coach yelled out: "Ladies! Looks like you want to start running track! GET IN THE GAME OR START RUNNING!"

Reba fought rolling her eyes. Does he really think that she wasn't doing anything on *purpose*? Well, maybe she was, but if she had any idea how to play or what was going on, she would most likely act like she was in the game like that other girl was doing.

"GIVE ME A GIRL QUARTERBACK FOR TEAM B!!!" Coach shouted.

Reba looked up, hoping that a girl on her team would be waving her hand widely, or at least waving her hand. But all the other girls, even the one that was pretending to play, also looked up hopefully.

"Alright then!" Coach yelled, "Who is number 17?" Reba's heart started beating fast as she slowly raised her hand.

"Shyner! You are the quarterback!" Coach yelled.

Reba hoped he would leave. But he didn't, he folded his arms over his chest like he does when he is staying for a while. Reba bit her lip and jogged over to her team mate holding the ball.

"What do I do?" Reba asked.

"Just catch the ball when I throw it to you, and then throw it to someone else," the boy said, Reba was pretty sure his name was Cole, but she wasn't positive, it was hard to be sure with new kids.

Then the boy crouched down and placed the football on the ground. About three lifetimes of awkward silence passed before the boy whispered, "say hike!"

"Hike!" Reba said.

The boy threw the ball to her. Reba caught it and looked around. A team mate half way across the field was waving his arms.

"Hey!" The boy hissed, he was only a few steps away from her. She tossed him the ball, and he began sprinting across the field.

"YES! GOOD JOB TEAM B! NOW LET'S GET A GIRL QUARTERBACK FOR TEAM A!" Coach yelled.

A girl raised her hand, and the game continued with Reba only having 3% more idea of what was going on. After the game Reba and the rest of her PE class went up to the lockers to change.

"Reba! Reba! Reeeeeeba!" Kat called as she jogged over .

"Reba!" Kat said loudly in Reba's ear.

"Ow! Hi Kat," Reba said, turning to Kat.

"Gosh, Reba! Sometimes I swear you are part deaf!" Kat joked but still looking irritated.

"Oh, heh heh, sorry," Reba said nervously, surprised at how accurate Kat was. "What were you saying?"

"I haven't said anything yet. But anyway I was going to ask you how your game went," Kat said, sounding more irritated.

"Oh, uh fine. I was the quarterback once," Reba said quickly.

"Me, too!" Kat said in a high pitched voice.

"Cool," Reba said. She wasn't surprised that Kat was a quarterback. Kat loved to be in the game, hated standing around watching someone else play when that could be her.

"How many times were you quarterback?" Kat asked as they approached the locker rooms.

"One time," Reba repeated.

"Only once? I was quarterback four times!" Kat said as she turned her lock to open her locker.

"Oh," Reba said as she pulled off her PE shirt and pulled on her shirt that she was wearing for the rest of the day.

At lunch Peyton babbled and babbled, talking about stuff that no one really cared about. Reba wasn't really listening to Peyton, after a while, none of her friends did either.

"And then Mr. Lavolonski told me that I had to meet him during lunch!" Peyton said rolling her eyes.

"Then shouldn't you go?" Abigail asked.

"Uh, seriously, you think I am going to spend my only free time during the school hours with *Mr. Lavolonski*?" Peyton asked, rolling her eyes again.

"Well, he asked you to," Abigail pointed out.

"Abby, I'm not going anywhere because someone asked me to. I do something because I *want* to," Peyton said, shoveling some spaghetti into her mouth, "So anyway…" Peyton continued to babble.

"Did you hear?" Reba heard Erin whisper to Brooke.

"I know right?" Brooke whispered out of the corner of her mouth.

"What?" Reba asked shyly.

"I'll tell you later," Erin promised.

Reba didn't like it when people said that to her because it was basically saying: "I don't want to tell you". But Reba knew that Erin would tell her; at least she hoped Erin would and wasn't just making up an excuse not to tell her.

After school Reba walked to the place that she and her friends met after school.

"'Kay bye!" Peyton called as soon as she saw Reba and fast walked to catch the bus.

"Bye bye!" Brooke said, giving everyone a hug and turning to where her older brother picks her up.

"See ya!" Abigail said, waving.

"Now is later," Erin said.

Reba felt a lot better knowing that Erin was a true friend. It was hard to tell who those were now days, but Reba knew how to tell.

"Well, did you hear about that new kid, Cole?" Erin asked.

"No," Reba said.

"He hangs out with Andy and Reese," Erin said hopefully.

"Uh," Reba blanked.

"Curly sandy hair, blue eyes?" Erin continued.

Reba realized that that description met the boy that had helped her in PE perfectly.

"Yah, I know who you mean," Reba said, snapping her fingers.

"Good," Erin said, nodding, "Well, he is like sticking up for the nerds and dorks! Can you believe it? Someone who is friends with Andy Koller has a soft spot for nerds!"

"Nerds?" Reba asked.

"Nerds. You know, Mitch Mathews, Steve Daily, and Collin Fellers? Smart, glasses wearing, shirt tucked in dorks?" Erin said.

"Collin doesn't wear glasses," Reba whispered. Did Collin really get teased a lot? Not that she cared of course. But she couldn't help feeling like she should do something about it.

"Duh! Don't you see him wearing those ugly thick glasses whenever he reads?" Erin pointed out.

"Oh, I guess not," Reba shrugged.

"Ya, and Cole is sticking up for them? How weird is that?" Erin asked.

"Very," Reba answered.

"Okay, bye!" Erin said, giving Reba a quick hug and then skipping away.

Reba looked around her at the deserted school grounds and began to slowly walk home.

The Football Injury:

✦

Collin

Collin carefully tucked in his shirt, patted down his pants, and smoothed his hair. Then placed his glasses in his shirt pocket.

"Are you ready yet, Collin?" his mother called up in her Texas tongue.

"Yes Mother!" Collin called back and jogged down the stairs, careful not to rumple his shirt.

"Let's go! You are going to be late!" his mother reminded him.

"Oh no!" Collin exclaimed and hopped in the car, making sure his seat belt was buckled. Collin arrived at school ten minutes early.

"Well, looks like you made it hon," She said as he hopped out.

Collin walked to where he met his friends.

"Collin! Hi!" Mitch called when Collin arrived.

"Hi, Mitch," Collin returned.

"Okay, so Collin, today you are going to ask Cole what he means okay?" Mitch ordered.

"What? NO!" Collin said, shaking his head.

"Yes!" Mitch said, shaking Collin's shoulders.

"Please don't do that!" Collin said, smoothing his shirt.

"Sorry, but we won't ever know unless you ask," Mitch said, crossing his arms.

"But why do I have to ask?" Collin asked.

"Because you went up to him before, so you should be the one to go again," Mitch explained, "Odd, Steve is usually here by this time."

Collin looked around and then checked his watch. Steve was no where in sight, and it was five minutes until the bell, Steve usually got here before Collin or a minute after.

"Hmm, maybe he will be late?" Mitch wondered.

"No, Antonio gets to school later than Steve, and he always makes it," Collin said, trying to get the subject as far away from Cole as possible.

"And Robert, well actually Robert waits outside his first period classroom every morning anyway," Mitch commented.

"Yeah, I wonder what Steve will do if he is sick?" Collin asked, trying to stall Mitch long enough until the bell so that he would forget about Cole.

"Probably make it up," Mitch said, shrugging and looked around for Steve again.

"So anyway," Mitch continued and Collin winced, "Find Cole; ask him what he meant, and then report back to us! Got it?"

"Yes," Collin sighed as he made sure his hair was in place.

"Spectacular," Mitch noted, then jumped when the bell rang.

Collin smiled and walked to class.

"And today in PE we will be doing flag football. Okay, go get dressed," Coach Fortman said.

Collin groaned, it was bad enough that Andy was in his class, but worse that he had to play football. He would probably make a fool of himself, giving Andy one more thing to tease him about. The worst part was that Cole wasn't in that class, so Andy would probably be giving him more put downs to make up for the times that Cole had stopped him.

Collin quickly changed into his ugly gray shorts and green school T-shirt. Collin quickly laced up his shoes, made sure his glasses and book were carefully stored in his locker, then he exited the locker room before Andy could find him. Andy wasn't in the exact same PE class as Collin, just the same period. Andy had Coach Winsted. There were three PE teachers: Coach Fortman, Coach Winsted, and Ms. Loyola. All of them did team sports together, which meant that Collin could be on the same team as Andy.

Collin shuddered as a cold breeze swept through his hair.

"Haha!" Collin turned and saw Andy with his cheeks puffed out.

"Hello," Collin greeted him.

Andy blew on Collin again. Collin winced as the cold air came straight at him; it was as cold as Andy's heart.

"Please stop," Collin commanded.

"Whatcha gonna do about it?" Andy asked.

Just then Coach Fortman called everybody over. "Alright now! Today we are playing flag football!" Coach Fortman roared, "Koller! Go back to your teacher!"

Andy jogged to Coach Winsted, making faces at Collin the entire time.

"Team A!" Coach Fortman bellowed. He called out all the people on Team A.

"B!" Coach Fortman called out the numbers for Team B.

"And the rest of you are Team C!" Coach Fortman yelled, "Down to the field!"

Collin stood up and dragged himself down to the field. He pulled on an orange flag and followed Coach Fortman's shaking finger to the last field.

"Alright! Team C will play against Coach Winsted's Team C!" Coach announced.

Collin looked up hopefully, and was relived to see Andy's angry face walking away from his team.

The rest of the game didn't go so well. Collin was too busy dodging the balls that were flying at him and trying to look tough.

"ROTATE!" Coach Fortman shouted. Collin's heart skipped a beat when he saw Andy Koller's smiling face walking toward him. Collin tried to swallow, but his throat was dry. He looked around him, but his team wasn't moving. Collin gulped as he let himself realize that he was playing against Andy.

Coach Winsted blew his whistle, and the game began.

Andy's team charged at Collin's team. A tall kid named Brandon threw the ball to a teammate that was waving his arms. Collin looked around and saw with envy that the girls were just standing around, doing nothing. Talking with their friends, or picking at their nails. None of them had to worry about being run over by Andy Koller.

Collin looked back to Andy and saw that Andy was almost five feet away from him. This brought fear to his legs, and they took off. He ran clear across the field, hoping his hair was staying down the entire time.

He suddenly felt something hard hit his head, and he fell to the ground. Collin struggled to keep his eyes open, to keep consciousness, but he was losing the battle. He gave up and his eyes closed. The last thing he saw was Andy Koller's smirking face.

"Collin? Collin baby?"

Collin's eyes cracked open and he saw his mother's smiling face. Her eyebrows were pulled together, making a concerned look on her face.

"Uh, hello mother," Collin said, confused, "I, uh, where am I?"

"Why you-"

"You are in the nurse's office," A lady wearing a white apron and rubber gloves interrupted his mother.

"Why?" Collin asked.

"A football injury," The nurse clarified.

"Oh, ow!" Collin exclaimed as he tried to sit up.

"No baby," Collin's mom said, gently pushing Collin down.

"How long have I been out?"

"I got here about three minutes ago," Collin's mother said, checking her watch.

"And it takes you three minutes to get here," Collin said, adding it up in his head.

"I was out for almost ten minutes!" Collin asked, horrified.

"No, I would say fifteen minutes minimum," The nurse answered, taking the icepack off his head and replacing it with a new one.

"Oh goodness!" Collin said.

"You got a nasty blow to the head you did," The nurse said.

"Well, I suppose I should bring him home," Collin's mom suggested.

"Yes, I suppose you should," The nurse said.

"Alright Collin," Collin's mother said, "Lets get you home."

Collin stood up with one hand pressing the ice pack to the purple lump that was growing out the back of his head. With the other hand he held onto his mother as they made their way to the car.

Revealing the Secret:

✦

Reba

"Here Reba," Brooke handed Reba a white envelope. It was a small envelope and had her name written in a purple gel pen on the front. All the rest of her friends were holding the same kind of envelope, so Reba didn't even have to open it to figure out she had been invited to Brooke's birthday party.

Reba tore open the envelope anyway, and sure enough, there in big puffy letters it said: "You're invited!" Reba opened the card and discovered it was a sleepover. Reba had never been to Brooke's house before because Brooke's parties were always at the beach or the mall. Erin was standing next to Brooke with her chin in the air. She had obviously helped Brooke make the invitations.

"Saturday? This Saturday?" Abigail asked when she opened her card.

"Yeah, why?" Brooke asked, looking worried. "You can go right?"

"Yes, but this is really short notice. I usually send out my invitations a month before my party so that no one makes any plans the day I have it," Abigail explained.

"Well she isn't you is she?" Kat accused, and then smiled to show that she was only kidding.

"So can you all make it?" Brooke asked, biting her lip.

"I got a soccer game from 11 to 12," Kat announced.

"But the party doesn't start until five," Brooke reminded her.

"Then I can go," Kat said, biting into her ham and lettuce sandwich.

"I can go," Peyton told her as she played with a strand of her hair.

"Reba? Can you go?" Brooke asked.

Reba usually said no to sleepovers, mainly because of the question "What is your deepest darkest secret?" and "Who do you have a crush on?" were the most common questions asked at sleepovers, and Reba didn't want to answer either of them. She didn't want to spill her deepest secret because her secret was that she was half deaf, and she could never think of a fake secret that was believable. She didn't want to spill her crush because she didn't have one, and when she told her friends that, they didn't believe her and pestered her to tell them.

But Reba was interested to see what Brooke's house looked like, so she said she could go.

"Wonderful!" Erin said, but before she or Brooke could begin talking about the party, Peyton began talking, and all hope of talking about the party was lost.

"Lily! Marie! I need your help!" Reba yelled as she banged on her older sisters' door.

"What?" The door flew open and Marie was standing there holding a curling iron in one hand and a lip pencil in another.

"I am going to a sleepover, and I need a fake crush and secret!" Reba ordered.

"Why do you need a fake crush? Why not tell your real one?" Marie asked.

"Because I don't have one!" Reba explained.

"Reba, even someone like you has a crush. Everyone has a crush," Marie said, rolling her eyes.

"But I don't!" Reba cried.

"Yes, you do! Now go away! I'm trying to get ready to go to the movies!" Marie ordered as she slammed the door in Reba's face.

"I'll help you lil' sister," Lily said from behind Reba.

Reba whirled around to find her older sister wearing a soccer jersey, sweat pants and socks, her usual outfit.

"Well, what do you need?" Lily asked. Reba quickly explained her situation to Lily.

"Why not tell them your real crush and secret?" Lily asked when Reba finished.

"Because I don't have a crush--"

"Or a secret?" Lily tried to finish for her. "C'mon Reba, everyone has a secret and a crush!"

"I do have a secret! But I can't tell them I am part deaf!"

"Why not?"

"What if they turn against me? I know Peyton can't keep her mouth closed, and my secret is too juicy for her to keep from telling the entire world!"

"Hmm, you could tell them something that isn't embarrassing, something that if Peyton told someone else, it wouldn't seem so bad," Lily pondered.

"But what?" Reba asked.

"Let's come back to that," Lily said, "Now your crush problem is easy. Just make sure someone else goes before you and say whatever that person says. That way your friends can't make fun of you for liking him."

"That is not bad advice," Reba said, nodding, "But what about the secret one?"

"When is this party?"

"Tomorrow."

"Shoot," Lily said, "Give me some time. I'll think of something."

Reba took a deep breath and pressed the doorbell. She heard music echo through the house, the deep bark of a dog, and Brooke's high pitched squeal.

The door flew open, and there Brooke stood her eyes full of excitement.

"Reba!" Brooke yelled as she struggled to take Reba's sleeping bag and suitcase.

"Its okay, I got it," Reba said as the small girl grabbed the present Reba was holding and pulled Reba into the house.

"Reba! How's it going?" Kat asked as she, Abigail, and Erin walked in.

"Fine, just fine," Reba answered.

"Fine? Well I'm GREAT!" Brooke said as she stretched her arms to show her happiness.

Then the doorbell rang, and Brooke flew to answer it.

Brooke returned skipping into the room followed by Peyton who was carrying a shiny blue suitcase.

"We are all here!" Brooke yelled.

"Okay, come on in!" Brooke's mother, Mrs. Chey, replied from Brooke's kitchen.

Reba and everyone else followed tiny Brooke into her humongous kitchen. Mrs. Chey looked a lot like Brooke in many ways. One way was height; Brooke's mom looked no taller than 5' 3". Mrs. Chey also had Brooke's wavy brown hair that swished from side to side when she walked. She had a dimple, and blue eyes, and, just like Brooke, unnaturally straight teeth.

"What is for dinner?" Kat asked licking her lips. Reba expected dinner to be pizza, because that was the main dish at all birthday parties.

"Make your own SUSHI!" Erin answered.

"I love sushi!" Abigail replied, clapping her hands.

"Yes! Me too!" Kat agreed.

"Sushi is so yummy! I always get it from this Japanese restaurant in Pasadena. The drive is a little long, but it is always so worth it! Like one time, my mom was having a party, and she wanted sushi, but there was a huge traffic jam-" Peyton yakked until Mrs. Chey interrupted.

"Line up to make your sushi," she called. Abigail's eyes grew wide, and Brooke blushed. No one ever interrupted Peyton for any reason. Peyton looked annoyed but quickly got over it since she knew she couldn't talk back to Mrs. Chey.

Reba made sure she was last in line for one reason: she hated sushi. She had tried it once before, and she had hated it so much. She couldn't stand the feeling of a dead fish with soy sauce swimming around in her mouth. But Reba decided to try it again and see if it was any better the second time around.

When it was Reba's turn, Reba only put in rice. It tasted even worse than her first sushi because it was so plain. Reba swallowed her bite and washed it down with a glass of soda. Then she mashed it up to look like she had eaten more than she really had.

Once everyone else finished their sushi, it was time for cake. Brooke had chosen a pure chocolate cake. Reba wolfed it down, even though she would have normally only eaten half of it because too much chocolate made her gag, but Reba was hungry from not eating her sushi, so she swallowed her entire slice of cake.

"Present time!" Erin sang after everyone finished their chocolate overload. Brooke clapped her hands as Mrs. Chey came in carrying an arm load of presents.

"Mom, can Buddy come in now?" Brooke begged.

"No sweetheart, once everyone is in their sleeping bags he can," Mrs. Chey answered as she grabbed a camera from a cabinet. "Say cheese!"

They all grinned, and Brooke's mom flashed the camera. Reba had no idea who Buddy was.

Brooke ripped the wrapping paper off a cube and squealed as she discovered it was a shirt. As Brooke opened the rest of her gifts, Reba discovered that Brooke did a lot of squealing, even for the boring presents she received like an almanac from her grandpa.

After presents, the girls watched *The Sisterhood of the Traveling Pants*. Reba didn't really like the movie because it was mostly about a bunch of girls getting boyfriends over the summer. She thought the part about the magic pants was kind of dumb because it was only magical because it fit all of the girls.

When the long movie finally finished, Kat, Abigail, Peyton, Erin, Brooke and Reba got ready for bed and climbed into their sleeping bags. They arranged the sleeping bags in a circle so they could whisper, and everyone else could still hear.

Just as Peyton opened her mouth to speak, the six girls heard a door open, and then the pounding of footsteps. Abigail swallowed noisily, and Kat looked around confused. Suddenly, a huge Bull Mastiff padded into the room and stood right over Brooke. It had a drop of drool hanging out the side of its mouth and was panting heavily.

"Buddy!" Brooke said as she sat up to hug her huge dog. Buddy sat down right next to Brooke, almost squashing Erin, but Erin rolled out of the dog's way just in time.

No one spoke for about 3 whole minutes. Reba fidgeted during the uncomfortable silence, wondering why no one had asked her her deepest darkest secret yet. But then Reba heard a door close, and Erin began talking.

"So," Erin said casually, "Who does everyone have a crush on?" Reba winced.

"Peyton, why don't you start?" Erin instructed.

"Okay," Peyton said, smiling. Reba bit her lip because she was right next to Peyton, which meant she was either last, or next. But it was probably best to be after Peyton anyways because when Reba named the same crush as her, Peyton couldn't make fun of Reba.

"I think Andy Koller is so cute!" Peyton said dreamily and then looked to Reba, which meant it was Reba's turn. Reba bit her lip again, Andy Koller was the last person on the planet she would ever have a crush on. Andy was extremely obnoxious, and he was really mean to people like Collin just because people like Collin were being themselves. But Reba had no other choice but to copy Peyton.

"I like Andy too," Reba sighed.

"As long as you don't ask him out, I'm fine with you and me having the same crush." Reba nodded and was relieved when Erin said her crush.

Once all of Reba's friends had confessed their crushes to the rest (which Reba was surprised to find out all were Andy or Reese), Erin asked Reba's second dreaded question.

"Since we are all besties and everything, we should know each other's deepest darkest secret," Erin said. "I'll go first. Well, I have to take these diarrhea pills every so often because when I eat a lot of sugar, I get super bad diarrhea."

Kat snorted.

"Be quiet! Why don't you tell your secret Miss Perfect Butt?" Erin shot at her.

"Well, I still don't wear a bra," Kat said, but she didn't seem embarrassed at all by it. Reba saw Peyton raised her eyebrows.

"Abby?" Kat asked.

"I, uh, I still play with Barbies," Abigail said, blushing deep crimson. Peyton raised her eyebrows again.

"We still love you," Brooke promised her.

"My mom is going to be a model and is moving to New York," Peyton said proudly. "And you better not tell anyone."

The girls promised not to.

"I have, um, I have ADD," Brooke whispered.

"That's not bad. It's just like having glasses," Erin assured her.

"How about you, Reba?" Erin asked.

"Well," Reba stalled, "My parents are getting divorced."

"Is that why your dad is never around?" Peyton asked. "Are you sure that is your biggest secret Reba? My parents are divorced, too."

Reba nodded. Her dad was actually dead. He died before she was born.

"Huh, so anyway I got some juicy gossip that you guys will love to hear!" Peyton promised. Reba smiled, relieved for her two dreaded questions to be behind her.

The Foot Sucking Dork:

Collin

"That's an unfortunate injury right there," Steve noted as he and Mitch examined Collin's bruise before school. The bruise stuck out of Collin's head like a third eye, it was every shade of purple with a splotch of blue here and there.

"How long do you think it will be there?" Mitch asked.

"The doctor said that as long as I keep ice on it, it should be gone soon," Collin informed.

"Does it still hurt?"

"Only when I touch it."

"Are you up for talking to Cole today?"

"No."

"Come on!" Mitch exclaimed. "You said that yesterday! When will you talk to Cole?"

"Never," Collin told him.

"Why not?"

"It is none of our business what his life was like before he came to this middle school!" Collin said.

"But we have a right to knowing stuff!"

43

"Mitch! Do. Not. Quote. Andy. Please!" Steve scolded.

"Sorry, but it is true! I am curious, and I really want to sleep tonight," Mitch announced.

"Why can't you sleep?"

"Because I am wondering what Cole meant!"

"Fine fine!" Collin gave up.

"Thanks, Buddy!"

The bell rang and they all left for class.

Collin saw Cole across the field after school , and if he had run he could have caught up to him. But Collin stayed rooted to the spot. For some reason he didn't want to talk to Cole. He knew Mitch would be mad; he knew Steve would get upset, but Collin just couldn't move his feet. His brain was sending signals for them to move, but his brain was also telling Collin to stay put. So Collin listened to the part of the brain that told him to stay and didn't move. He did move actually. He moved in the direction that went away from Cole. Collin walked far away from Cole to where Collin's mother was.

"What do you mean *he was too far away?*" Mitch shrieked the next day at lunch when Collin told his friends the events of the day before.

"I just couldn't reach him in time," Collin lied.

"You have got to ask him, Collin!" Mitch ordered.

"I know I know," Collin muttered.

"Why don't you ask him now?" Robert asked.

"Now?" Collin turned to see Cole walking to the bathroom.

"Yes! Now!" Steve urged.

"I don't know…" Collin said.

"Hurry!" Mitch said and he pushed Collin in Cole's direction.

Collin walked to Cole but began to jog after his friends started hissing at him to do so.

"Cole!" Collin called when he was a few feet behind him. Cole didn't turn but went straight into the bathroom. Collin began to return to his friends, but Steve and Mitch both motioned him to stay.

When Cole came out, Collin blocked his exit with a friendly smile.

"Hello Cole!" Collin greeted him.

"Uh, hi…" Cole said blankly.

"Collin, my name is Collin and I-" Collin started but a grip on his shoulder stopped him.

"Cole isn't stupid *Collin*," Andy interrupted.

"But he-"

"Butt nothing! Cole isn't stupid! Besides, who would want to know *your* name anyway?" Reese asked.

"Exactly bro, who cares who a loser's name is?"

"Only a foot sucking dork!"

"You got that right! Can you name any kids who care what his name is?"

"Uh yeah! Let's see, there is Steve, and Mitchell, and Robert and Antonio!"

"Don't make fun of my friends!" Collin demanded.

"Aww! How sweet!" Andy snorted.

"Really! Stop!" Collin pleaded. Collin met Cole's eyes; Cole looked away quickly as if looking at Collin might hurt him.

"Since you care what your friends' names are, that makes you a foot sucking dork as well!" Andy accused as he nudged Cole. "Right Cole! Tell Collin how big of a dork he and Steve and Mitchell and Robert and Antonio are! Tell him!"

"But I don't know all those people you named except Collin, so I can't answer that," Cole replied.

Collin expected Andy to call Cole a dork, or look at Cole with a disapproving expression, but Andy only looked hopeful.

"They are those guys over there," Andy gestured to where Collin's friends were sitting. "Just by glancing at them, you can easily tell they are dorks!"

"No, it is hard for me to tell," Cole said. "Listen, the bell is going to ring soon, and I still have to finish my lunch." Cole walked right past Collin to the lunch tables, Andy and Reese at his heels.

Collin returned to his friends, who had witnessed the entire thing. Mitch's face glowed.

"Please don't say 'I told you so'," Collin begged of Mitch.

Mitch nodded, but his face said it all.

The Dreaded Hearing Aid:

✦

Reba

It had been a week since Brooke's slumber party, and Reba had a bigger problem on her hands: her hearing had gotten worse. Her only working ear was starting to go deaf, so much that Reba had to skip school. Reba could only hear if you were standing right next to her and speaking really loudly.

Reba was mortified. *What is wrong with me?* She thought. She wasn't supposed to loose her hearing at age 13. No no, hearing was supposed to leave at around age 70 or 80. In an attempt to make Reba feel better, Reba's mother told Reba that she must be maturing extremely fast. Of course this didn't help at all because no one matures to sixty years more than their age.

"What are we going to do?" Reba sobbed. She knew what was coming was what she didn't want to hear, well, she could barely hear it if her mother told her. But her mother told her it anyway. Even though Reba was crying into a pillow on the couch and her mother was standing across the room, Reba could hear her mother's answer perfectly clear.

"I guess you will need a hearing aid," Her mother said shrugging.

"No! No! I can't Mom! I can't!" Reba wailed. "What about surgery? That is an option! It is!"

"Honey, there isn't surgery for that," Mrs. Shyner said.

"I. Can't. Get. A. Hearing. Aid!" Reba sobbed. "I'M ONLY 13!!!"

"Relax! I bet they have a kind you will like. You cannot miss another day of school Reba; we are getting this hearing aid Today!" Mrs. Shyner said, pulling Reba off the couch and guiding her into the car.

Reba sat on the smooth leather seats in silence. She couldn't believe this was happening to her. Her mother was on the phone, probably calling the hearing aid people, as she drove. Reba saw people angrily honking their horns at the lady who was talking on her cell phone while driving, but Reba didn't hear a sound.

A knot was growing bigger and tighter in Reba's stomach.

Mrs. Shyner pulled into the hearing aid people's parking lot and pulled Reba off the smooth leather car seat and into the office. When Reba went in, the waiting room was empty. Reba's mother whispered something to her, but Reba couldn't hear her.

"What?" Reba asked loudly.

Mrs. Shyner looked embarrassed, and said something to the thin secretary.

The secretary led Mrs. Shyner and Reba through a door and into a cramped office. A bald man with a red goatee stood there with a clip board. He smiled and said something, but of course, Reba couldn't hear it.

"What?" Reba asked loudly again.

The man looked surprised, and pointed to his name tag. His name tag read: *Dr. Kenne*. Reba nodded.

"I'm Reba," Reba said.

"Not so loud Reba," Mrs. Shyner said loud enough for Reba to hear. Reba's eyebrows knitted together, she hadn't tried to be loud.

Dr. Kenne said something to Mrs. Shyner, and the two started a conversation that was probably at normal volume, but Reba couldn't hear a word of it. Mrs. Shyner pulled out some papers and showed them to Dr. Kenne. Dr.Kenne nodded and pushed his glasses higher up his nose.

He handed Reba a pair of headphones and motioned for Reba to put them on. Reba struggled to not roll her eyes. *I may be deaf, but I'm not stupid!* Reba thought as she put on the headset. Dr. Kenne walked over to his computer and pressed a few buttons. Then he shouted, "Raise you hand when you hear something! Raise the hand that is the same side as the ear you hear it!" Reba nodded.

The headphones threw a bunch of sounds at her like the 's' sound and the 'g' sound. Reba raised the same hand every time she heard any faint sound. When the test finally finished, Dr. Kenne and Mrs. Shyner talked and talked. Dr. Kenne kept pointing at the computer screen with his pen. Finally, he brought out a case of hearing aids.

"This one is a CIC. It is the smallest," Dr. Kenne shouted, handing Reba a tiny hearing aid.

Dr. Kenne demonstrated how to put it in, and Reba learned quickly. She turned on the hearing aid and pushed it far into her ear. Dr. Kenne's lips moved, but no sound came out. Then suddenly, Reba could hear! Only in the ear that she could hear in before though.

"Can you hear me? Well, I guess the CIC isn't strong enough, let's try this one," Dr. Kenne said.

"No no! I can hear you! I can!" Reba cut in.

"Really?" Dr. Kenne questioned.

"Yes! Everything is just like it used to be! Can I have another one for my other ear?" Reba begged.

"Reba, your hearing loss in your other ear is pretty severe, either that or you were born deaf. To hear out of your other ear would require a bigger hearing aid," Mrs. Shyner explained quietly. Reba nodded and smiled.

"Do you have any we can buy right now?" Reba's mother asked Dr. Kenne.

"Actually, I do!" Dr. Kenne said as he pulled out a couple more boxes.

"How much will that be?" Mrs. Shyner asked.

The grownups continued their conversation, and Reba heard every word crystal clear.

Covered in Lunch:

Collin

"No! NO!" Collin shouted after school at Mitch.

"Collin! C'MON!!" Mitch begged.

"I refuse to communicate with Cole again! I will not! If you want to find out his secret so badly, then why don't YOU go ask him?" Collin hissed.

"Because you--"

"Because I started this whole thing? But I am not the person who is losing sleep over it!"

"Yes, but what would Cole think if--"

"You want to know, Mitch, not me. I just want to be out of it!" Collin cried.

"Humph!" Mitch gave up, defeated.

"Yes," Collin smiled.

Then Mitch did too, "But, you *do* want to know. Maybe not as much as I do, but you want to know."

Collin wrinkled his eyebrows. Of course he was curious to know what Cole was hiding, but he, like Mitch, didn't want to be the one to find it out. Going up to Cole was like going up to a spy at war on the opposing side; you think the spy is on your side, but when you get close enough to ask, the soldiers on the spy's side blast you away with bullets, or in Collin's case, they blasted him away with words.

"Here is a deal. We go together," Mitch compromised

"I never said I wanted to know," Collin defended himself.

"But I know you do! I may not have straight A's like you, Collin, but I can easily figure out that you are curious!" Mitch said, slapping Collin on the back.

"Oh my! Mitch, you rumpled my shirt!" Collin quickly tried to smooth down his shirt.

"We will go tomorrow!" Mitch declared.

Mitch and Collin hid behind a trash can the next day at lunch. Mitch stuck his head out cautiously.

"Mitch, is this really necessary?" Collin inquired.

The bottoms of his pants were already getting wet and the ground behind the trashcan was filthy. When Collin brought his hands to his face, tiny balls of dirt rolled off his palms.

"Mitch!" Collin hissed to get his friend's attention.

"Shh! don't blow our cover!" Mitch hissed back. "Cole is getting up. Prepare to approach."

Collin peeked around the trashcan and saw Cole wrapping up his lunch and throwing it away in a trashcan behind Cole. Cole stood up and brushed some crumbs off his pants. Collin waited eagerly for Cole to stand up and walk far enough away from Andy and Reese so that Collin and Mitch could talk to Cole. Cole and Mitch had planned it all out. They would promise not to spill any secrets and to not say a word to anyone other than Steve, Robert and Antonio. Cole was almost around the corner. Collin's heart bounced in his chest, and Collin turned to nudge Mitch, but Mitch wasn't there.

Before Collin had time to look around for Mitch, something gooey and wet hit his head. A cold liquid trickled down Collin's nose. Collin sniffed and realized it was a type of soda. Collin looked up to see Andy, who was making a face of false worry.

"Oh I'm sorry, guess I missed the trashcan. You shouldn't hide behind trashcans like that Collin, or else things like this can happen," Andy said, his words overflowing with mock caring.

Collin quickly stood up; a lunch tray slid off his head, following the lunch tray came a soda can (now empty after its contents spilled all over Collin), a half eaten pizza, and an unfinished Popsicle. Collin's hands flew to his head. They came back covered in sticky melted Popsicle remains, pizza sauce, and soda.

Collin was horrified and fought tears as he rushed to the bathroom. As Collin turned the corner to the bathroom, he saw Mitch and Cole. Cole was saying something to Mitch, but Collin didn't stop to hear it.

As soon as Collin arrived in the bathroom, he forced out as many paper towels as he could out of the paper towel dispenser and forced his head under the water faucet. He scrubbed and tried over and over to get the remains of Andy's lunch out of his hair, but with no success. Collin finally gave up and decided to go home and take a shower; he would take it quickly so that he could get back in the middle of fifth period.

Collin ran to the nurse's office and called his mom, telling her to get here as quickly as she could. His mother took him home, and he showered quickly. Then he grabbed some clean clothes and jumped back in the car. He arrived back at school the same time he had planned: the middle of fifth period.

"Well, what did you find out?" Collin asked Mitch the next morning after he had finished explaining why he had left.

"Uh, nothing," Mitch said, biting his lip and avoiding Collin's eyes.

Collin was not fooled by Mitch's response. Perhaps if Mitch had looked disappointed and ordered Collin to go after Cole again, Collin would have been fooled. But Collin could easily tell that Mitch knew and didn't want to tell.

"You did too find out something!" Collin accused. "I got covered in Andy's lunch to find out the outcome of this mystery!"

"Well, sacrificing doesn't make the answer come! I didn't find out anything that would help *you*," Mitch said defensively.

"Aha! So you did find out something! I will tell Steve this, and then you will be forced to tell! Steve will get it out of you, no doubt! In fact, here he comes now!" Collin said triumphantly as Steve strolled over to them.

"Good morning," Steve greeted them.

"Steve, Mitch found out Cole's secret! He found out and doesn't want to tell us!" Collin accused. Collin felt cheerful knowing that the truth was so close to being figured out.

"Well, uhm, I'm sure Mitch has good reason for keeping this secret from you," Steve mumbled, not looking Collin in the eye. Collin noted that Steve said 'keeping this secret from you', not 'keeping this secret from us'.

Collin gasped, "You know, don't you! Hey guys, now that isn't fair! Why can't I know?"

Steve and Mitch were silent. Collin realized that Steve didn't deny that he knew.

"And Robert and Antonio know too?" Collin asked.

Steve and Mitch did nothing.

"Oh goodness! I am the only one!" Collin moaned.

"Calm down Collin, I'm sure that if you ever found out you would be happy to not know. Besides, Cole didn't tell me everything and made me promise not to tell you. If I tell you, then he might not tell me the rest, or you would want to know and go find him and demand to know, and then he would know I told," Mitch explained desperately.

"Well I'm sure you are dying to know too, I wouldn't mind waiting until he told you more," Collin compromised. "What did he say?"

"Well, the thing is, we don't know what it means," Steve said.

"Excuse me? Did he speak in a foreign language or in code? HOW COULD YOU NOT KNOW WHAT IT MEANS?!" Collin cried.

"Well, he only said a few words and then left because Andy and Reese were coming," Mitch said.

"Why were Andy and Reese coming?"

"To give me my daily dose of verbal abuse."

"Oh," Collin sighed, "What did he say?"

"He said his full name was Nicolas Henry Johnson, but that's it," Mitch said. "Do you know what that means?"

Collin shook his head. But something in his head clicked. Something that would take a lot of digging to uncover.

The Crush's' Pranks:

Reba

Reba loved her hearing aid. She could hear everything crystal clear in her only working ear. Though some things she didn't want to hear, like the details in her cousin's foot surgery or Peyton talking about how funny it was when Andy dumped his lunch on Collin's head (Reba felt bad for Collin, unlike her heartless friends, but had tried to push away the feeling because no one cared what happened to a dork, so why should she?), Reba was happy to hear anything at all.

"And then did you see the look on Collin's face? Oh it was hilarious!" Peyton giggled for the fifth time that day.

Reba was surprised that her own friends were actually paying attention to what Peyton had to say. In fact, her friends and Peyton were actually conversing over the subject of Andy pranking Collin! And laughing and smiling! True blue having-a-good-time-no-wait-the-best-time-of–my-life smiles! So Collin's pain and all the others that Reba's friends classified as dorks' pain made them HAPPY? Reba could not believe it! How on earth did she become friends with these people? Reba would rather have no friends than be friends with people who had hearts made of volcanic rock. No wait, being friends with these people is more than a thousand times better than having no friends.

Having no friends, no one to eat lunch with or talk to or cry with, is like a bottomless pit of hurt and sadness. It swallows you up and tells you how much of a loner you are. Reba knew this feeling too well. Reba's fourth grade friendship may have been bad, but Reba's fifth grade friendship was the worst. In fourth grade she still sat with SOMEONE at lunch. In fifth grade, she would have had a higher social status if she had been an empty gum wrapper on the street. No one even glanced at her or realized she was there. Every day at lunch she fought tears when she sat alone at an empty lunch table and ate her boloney sandwich.

You may be wondering how Reba came to this state. Well allow me to explain. On the first day of first grade, Reba arrived at Sea Spring Elementary for her second time. She made friends with a girl who had dark hair and green eyes. This girl was named Marisa. Marisa and Reba became close friends, sharing laughs and playing in Marisa's kiddie pool. By second grade, the girls were best friends. But in the summer before fourth grade, Marisa unexpectedly moved to England because her mother's work was moving. Reba only had two days' notice. She didn't even get to say good bye to Marisa. Reba hadn't seen Marisa since.

Reba was smart, and in the first week of fourth grade, Reba walked up to a group of girls and asked to sit with them. Reba had expected them to be happy and inviting and introduce themselves to her and make her feel even the tiniest bit welcome, but they only looked at her and shrugged and continued their dull conversation. Reba had tried to push herself into their group, tried to stick up for herself when they left while she threw her trash away or snickered at their inside joke without even saying it was an inside joke, but her attempts were laughable. Reba would never give up on making friends, and these girls seemed to be her only shot. But on the second day of fifth grade, the leader of the group, Ellen, had walked up to her and asked her to leave her and her friends alone. The exchange of words had happened like this:

Ellen: "Rachel-"

Reba: "Reba."

Ellen: "Whatever. I speak for all of my friends when I tell you that I don't want you to eat lunch with us anymore, or follow us around. You are super annoying and stupid for not realizing sooner that no one likes you, or ever will. So if you could please go away and not bother us ever again, we would appreciate it."

Ellen had left Reba heart broken and shocked. She bit her lip and ran away as Ellen returned to her circle of friends.

Reba had spent the rest of her fifth grade career wandering the play ground alone, studying by herself, and crying at night. Reba was miserable. The dark pit had swallowed her up and had whispered in her ear that she would never have friends and would always be a loner. Ellen's words echoed in her head: "You are annoying and stupid for not realizing that no one likes you or ever will." Reba believed those words for a whole grade, until she realized that she had to snap out of it before she committed suicide.

In sixth grade (Reba was in middle school now because her middle school started in sixth grade), Reba had walked up to Brooke and Erin and Kat and Abigail. She had asked them if she could eat lunch with them. They had done everything Reba had expected her first group of 'friends' to do. They smiled and nodded. They asked her her name and told her theirs. They had given her the spotlight. She had been the center of attention. They had told each other everything about each other. Then, in the middle of the year, Peyton had come. Erin, Brooke, Kat and Abigail had known Peyton before and were excited to see her again. Erin had explained that Peyton had been at their school in third grade but had left in fifth grade to live in Utah with her mom. Now Peyton was back, and as accepting as Erin, Brooke, Kat and Abigail had been, Reba had felt like she had a home for the first time in years.

"Reba?" Kat asked snapping.

Reba returned to her circle of friends from her day dreaming.

Then Kat said her famous line to Reba, "Gosh, sometimes I swear you are part deaf."

"And then my favorite part was when Collin stood up and had that LOOK on his face!" Peyton laughed. *How many times has she said that? 16? 17? 50?* Reba thought.

"So you liked that prank, huh?"

All the girls turned around to see Andy and Reese, but no Cole. Andy's brown hair threatened to turn to dreadlocks, and Reese's wild black hair was only seen before on a rock star.

Reba saw Peyton's eyes light up, and her cheeks turned rose.

"Oh yes! It was the funniest thing I have ever seen!" Peyton replied as she and everyone else except Reba stood up so that they didn't have to look up to see Andy's face.

"I liked the prank when you took Collin's glasses and hid them for a day and told him a bird had picked them up. Oh his face was the best!" Kat said to Reese, smiling.

Next thing Reba knew, all her friends were telling their crush (which was either Andy or Reese) their favorite prank that their crush did. Reba was shocked that a majority of them were on Collin.

"You girls are in luck," Andy said to Peyton, "because I and Reese here are planning a prank on Collin. When Reese and I finish planning you can tell whoever you want to come see Collin be more embarrassed than he has ever been! Just make sure the people you tell won't tell Collin."

Reba was horrified, and for a brief second expected her friends to be the same. But no:

"Oh we will NOT miss that!" Peyton promised.

Reba's heart sunk.

The Preschool Yearbook:

✦

Collin

"Collin! Come here!" Collin's mother called.

Collin groaned. He was studying for his science exam, and wanted to do superb on it. But constant interruptions like the phone and the television caused him to forget the information he put in his brain less than a few seconds before.

"Collin! Come here! I found something!" Collin's mother called again.

Collin reluctantly left his science book on his desk and shuffled down the hall to his mother.

"Yes?" Collin asked impatiently.

"I found a whole bunch of stuff from when you were a baby!" His mother chirped.

"Oh. I am going to go study again," Collin said, turning to leave.

"No no! Studying can wait! Look at this stuff with me! It is adorable!" His mother grabbed Collin's shirt and pulled him back. Collin sat down abruptly and figured there was no use arguing with his mother.

"Oh look! Here is one of you and Reba! Remember her? You two used to be such good friends," Collin's mother sighed.

Collin remembered all too well and took the picture of him and Reba his mother handed him. The scene was Reba's birthday party. Reba had a mouthful of cake and had her arm around Collin's shoulder. Reba looked no older than three, but Collin would recognize her anywhere, even with a face covered in frosting. Reba's reddish-brown hair was cropped short, and Collin's blonde hair was not smoothed down like it is now.

"Oh! Here is your preschool yearbook! I think your preschool was the only one that had a yearbook! It was just like elementary! They took pictures of each and every one of you kids! That is hilarious!" Collin's mother giggled as she flipped through the preschool yearbook.

Collin looked longingly down the hall were his science book was waiting to be memorized.

"Oh there's you!" Collin's mother chuckled, pointing at a scrawny, glasses-less, and younger version of Collin.

"Here, look at it," Collin's mother said, handing it to him.

"I think I will take it into my room and look there," Collin said, grabbing the yearbook and returning to his science book.

Collin studied for three hours straight before he was called down for dinner. After dinner Collin took a shower, finished up his geography homework, and read his book for English. The minute hand on the clock hit 12, bringing the hour hand over the 9.

"Time for bed!" Collin's mother called.

Once in bed, Collin grabbed his book and began to read where he left off. Collin always read in bed to make him sleepy. But to Collin's disappointment, he had finished the book the night before and had nothing to read.

Collin scanned his room for something to read. His eyes rested on the preschool yearbook, and he snatched it up.

Collin flipped through the yearbook. Pictures of toddlers filled up every page, most of whom, Collin didn't remember. But

Collin did recognize some pictures: his own, Reba's, the mean teacher's, the janitor's, the trouble maker's, the nice teacher's. Collin finished looking at the pictures, and since he wasn't tired yet, he decided to look at the names of the children to see if he knew any now.

Collin had no luck until one name caught his eye: Nicolas Henry Johnson.

Collin's heart beat fast, and he desperately looked at the picture of Nicolas to be sure there was no confusion. But even in a black and white photo, piercing blue eyes shot out of the page, sandy curls bounced every which way.

It was Cole.

So Cole went to Collin's preschool. That didn't mean anything. Collin never interacted with Cole at the preschool, or had he?

Two Sticks of Butter:

Reba

"Reba! Phone!" Mrs. Shyner called from downstairs.

Reba turned up her hearing aid and scrambled down the stairs. It was always harder for her to hear people on the phone. Reba snatched the phone from the hook and pressed it against her ear.

"Hello?" Reba asked into the receiver.

"Reba! It's Abigail!" Abigail's voice chimed into Reba's ear loud and clear.

"Hi Abby! What's up?"

"I'm inviting everyone over for a barbeque!" Abigail announced.

"Great! What time?"

"4:30 this afternoon!"

"Oh, let me ask my mom," Reba covered the mouthpiece with her hand and called over her shoulder.

"Mom! Mom!" Reba called.

"Yes?" Mrs. Shyner asked.

"Can I go over to Abigail's at 4:30 this afternoon?"

"Sounds good to me," Reba's mother said.

"My mom said yes! I'll see you then!" Reba said into the phone.

"Brilliant! And could you bring a dish too? It is sorta like a potluck," Abigail said quickly.

"Okay, sure," Reba replied.

"Great! Bye!" And the line went dead.

It was 4 o'clock. Reba grabbed her jacket and her shoes. Then, she catapulted herself down the carpeted stairs into her kitchen. She had completely forgotten to make a dish for Abigail's party. She scanned the shelves of her pantry for something that could be made in less than half an hour. The only thing in the pantry was a box of macaroni and cheese, a loaf of bread, and a box of cereal.

Reba sighed and slammed the pantry door. Her mother was out grocery shopping and wouldn't be back for at least an hour. The fridge had similar results to the pantry. The inventory of the fridge was an almost empty jar of jam and a jug of milk with no more than half a serving left in it. Reba panicked. She wanted to contribute to the potluck badly, but with her home without food, she couldn't. She decided to make the macaroni and cheese.

Reba discovered with a sigh that macaroni and cheese required butter, but she didn't have any.

"Marie! We are all out of butter! I need some for the party!" Reba yelled to her sister.

"Go ask a neighbor for some then!" Marie yelled back.

Reba didn't want to go outside and disturb a neighbor for a stick of butter. She glanced at the clock and jumped when the clock read 4:15 pm. Reba tied her shoes onto her feet and zipped her jacket up her chest. Glancing out the window, Reba saw all her neighbors' houses.

Reba made a mental list of her neighbors in her head and looked at each house for an excuse to cross it off her list. The Johnstones were in Hawaii. Scratch them off. Mr. Oleyday was too grouchy and probably wouldn't give her butter anyway. The Rickson's car wasn't in the driveway so they probably went out to dinner. That only left the Fellers. Collin Fellers and his mother.

Reba gulped; she hadn't made eye contact with Collin in a long time. Longer than she could remember. But he was the only house left.

Reba stepped out onto her porch . She walked slowly to Collin's house but remembering her time crunch made her speed up. Reba pressed her finger against the doorbell and listened to the chimes echoing in the house. Reba waited, almost hoping no one would be home so she could avoid and awkward conversation with Collin, or maybe his mother would answer the door.

Before Reba could get her hopes up, the door opened, and there stood Collin; his hair combed down and parted neatly, his shirt tucked in, and his glasses case poked out of his chest pocket.

He looked surprised to see her, but smiled quickly.

"Reba! What a surprise! How may I assist you?" he asked.

Reba pushed her reddish-brown hair behind her ear and made eye contact with Collin for the first time in years.

"I was wondering if I could borrow a couple sticks of butter. Well not borrow, because I'm not giving them back because I am going to use them when I cook," Reba stuttered.

"Oh! Of course! I'll return in a moment!" Collin agreed before he disappeared.

Reba was surprised at how polite Collin was. She fidgeted with her zipper until he returned with three sticks of butter.

"Thanks," Reba mumbled as she took the butter from Collin.

"You're welcome!" Collin nodded and Reba turned to make her journey back to her kitchen.

When Reba entered her home the clock read 4:28. Reba scrambled into the kitchen and grabbed a cooking pot. She filled it with water and set it to a boil. She did the rest of the procedure quickly, causing her macaroni and cheese to finish five minutes early. Reba didn't even care, she was panicking because the clock read 4:45 by the time the macaroni and cheese finished. She shoved oven mitts onto her hands and grabbed the pot of macaroni.

"I need a ride to Abigail's!" Reba called. No answer.

She flung open Marie and Lily's bedroom door. Marie and Kevin sat on Marie's bed and were watching a movie on the TV in the twin's room. Kevin looked bored out of his mind, but Marie's eyes were huge as she carefully ate the popcorn in her lap. She tore her eyes away from the screen to look at Reba.

"What?" she asked.

"Where is Lily?" Reba asked.

"At her lacrosse game."

"Oh, well can you give me a ride to Abigail's?" Reba asked hopefully.

"No," Marie said firmly.

"Please! You can have all of my make up!"

Marie's brow scrunched up as she looked down at her skin tight jeans.

"No way. I don't need any six year old princess lip gloss thank you very much!" Marie replied.

"How about my curling iron! You can have that for keeps!" Reba tried.

"Fine!" Marie sighed as she paused the TV and grabbed her keys.

Reba followed her downstairs gratefully and grabbed her macaroni.

Kevin, Marie and Reba piled into Marie's cherry red car. The car was also Lily's because the twins shared it.

Marie sped down every block and made sharp turns at every corner. Reba quietly said directions, and Marie barked for them to be louder. Marie finally pulled up in front of Abigail's house. Reba hopped out and shyly thanked Marie for the ride. Marie sniffed in return and sped back home.

Reba carefully walked up to Abigail's door and knocked on it. Both of Abigail's parents opened the door. Though they looked like Abby, their attitudes were nothing like Abigail's. Abigail's mom was thin and tall with a flower clip embedded in her poofy yellow hair. Abigail's dad was thin also, but his hair was chocolate brown.

"Ah, Reba! Welcome! It was getting so late we were wondering if you were coming at all!" Abigail's mother said as she lifted a long and lean hand to usher Reba inside.

Abigail's mother's words were a perfect example of how different Abigail was from her parents. Abigail was very nice and would never say something so rude.

"What did you bring?" Abigail's father asked as he peeked into Reba's pot. "Oh, macaroni. Not nearly as exciting or delicious as what your friends brought." Another example of Abigail's difference from her parents.

Reba finally got out to the backyard and found the table with the food on it. Abigail's father was right. Reba set her macaroni and cheese down next to a chocolate devil's food cake and Gnocchi (Reba only knew it was Gnocchi because of the name tag). Reba looked at the rest of the food on the table. She saw elegant soups and delicious home made pie.

"Reba! Glad you could make it!" Abigail greeted Reba with a smile that sent a thousand bolts of friendliness.

"Glad I am here!" Reba responded with a smile she hoped was close to Abigail's.

"Reba! Hey! We all want to play hide and seek, but Peyton says it is too babyish. Will you help us convince her?" Kat asked as she appeared at Abigail's side.

"What did you bring?" Reba asked.

"I brought Chilean Dobladitas with jam and butter," Kat said breezily as she pointed at her dish.

"Where is it from?" Reba asked as her nose smelled the irresistible scent of the Chilean Dobladitas.

"South America. Now c'mon!" Kat said impatiently.

"Oh."

The three girls walked over to Peyton who was shaking her head with her eyes closed at a tiny Brooke.

"No no no no no! I am not going to go hide in the bushes and act like I am five years old!" Peyton declared.

"Then let's make it more interesting!" Kat suggested. "First person to be found, or first loser has to prank Andy Koller, and second loser has to prank call Reese!"

"Great! Let's roll a die to pick who counts!" Brooke suggested.

They all rolled. Erin ended up being the counter. Lucky for Reba, she wasn't first or second loser and didn't have to prank call anyone.

On the second round, Abigail made a good point, "They probably won't pick up the phone if we prank call them again. We need to pick new people."

"Okay. First loser has to prank call Steve Daily and second loser has to prank call, uhm, who is that kid with the black hair and is really over weight?" Kat asked.

"Robert Cohen?" Peyton offered.

"Yes him. Second loser has to prank call Robert Cohen," Kat nodded.

Reba was thankful that she was counting that round and once again wouldn't have to call anyone.

At the third round, they switched the victims of the prank calls again.

"Mitch Mathews for first loser and Collin Fellers for second," Kat announced as everyone scrambled to hide.

Reba hid behind a bush and held her breath. She heard Erin tell Brooke that she had found Brooke. Reba tried to be as quiet as possible, but Erin found her second. Now Reba was going to be the one to prank call poor Collin. Reba knew it was coming. You knew it was coming too, didn't you, Reader?

Once everyone was found and Brooke finished pretending to be a radio show host, Reba numbly picked up the phone and dialed the phone number Kat handed her. She didn't want to disturb Collin, but there was nothing she could do.

"Hello?" Collin's boyish voice rang out of the speaker phone. All the prank calls made that day were on speaker phone so that the whole group could hear the conversation.

"Hi," Reba said in her normal voice. Kat made a face at her to change her voice.

"Reba? Is that you?" Collin asked. *How on earth did he recognize my voice?* Reba thought. Her friends were as bewildered as she was.

"No, I'm, uh," Reba stuttered as she made her voice go higher. Peyton scribbled something on a piece of paper. It read 'Connie Williams. Sweepstakes.'

"Hello? Hello? Reba? Who is this?" Collin asked.

"No, not Reba, Connie Williams," Reba said quickly in the same high pitched voice.

"I don't know any Connie William's ma'am," Collin replied.

"I'm from, uhm, a sweepstakes," Reba stuttered.

"A sweepstakes? I didn't enter any sweepstakes," Collin's voice was confused.

"Uh," Reba looked to her friends for help. Suddenly, Kat pushed Reba out of the way and imitated Reba's high pitched voice.

"Sorry, I am her twin sister, Amelia Williams. You have just won a vacation to Washington DC, and a life time supply of sunscreen and scented hand lotion," Kat said.

"I'm sorry, I believe you have the wrong person," Collin suggested.

"Is this not 933-0008?" Kat asked.

"No. This is 933-0008," Collin replied.

"And are you the man of the house, Collin Fellers?" Kat furthered.

"Yes. But how did I win?" Collin asked.

"Do you go to James Middle School?" Kat asked.

"Yes."

"We got permission from your Principal Karey to enter all the students' names and phone numbers into the sweepstakes who had perfect grades, and your name was drawn."

"Why wasn't I alerted of this?"

"Ever heard of a surprise?"

"Yes."

"We will send the tickets and sunscreen and lotion to your door. Have a beautiful day!"

"You too, Miss!"

Kat hung the phone on the hook and beamed.

"That was the best one yet! Great job, Kat!" Everyone congratulated Kat with smiles and pats on the back.

"How about I prank call a few more? Then we eat?" Kat suggested. Everyone nodded, except Reba who was too ashamed that she hadn't stopped the prank calls. Reba knew she should have stopped Kat as she prank called random people from the school directory saying Kat was a pizza woman, or a super model, or a hippie.

Kat finally finished and everyone giggled as they headed for the food table to grab random food from the table (except Reba because she had not thought it was funny to tease anyone), not even looking at what they were grabbing because they assumed it was all delicious. Reba bit her lip as Peyton subconsciously dished some of Reba's macaroni onto her plate and laughed.

Reba picked up a plate and took some of Kat's Chilean Dobladitas with jam and butter and her own macaroni. Then she sat at the table with her friends.

Everyone was still laughing when Reba sat down.

"I liked the one Kat did to Collin! That was so hilarious!" Erin laughed. Everyone laughed with her, including Reba. Reba didn't think it was funny, but she wanted her friends to think she had a good sense of humor.

"Hey! I have an idea! What if we really do send him sunscreen and lotion!" Erin suggested.

"Oh that would be so funny!" Brooke chuckled.

"Yah! We could send him one tube of sunscreen and one of those little bottles of lotion you get from hotels! We could send him a picture of Washington DC and tell him to imagine he is there! It would be so funny!" Erin continued.

Everyone (except Reba) thought it was a great idea and agreed to do it after they ate. Reba looked down at her macaroni; the cheese was clumped together, and the noodles were soggy. Reba bit into a spoon full of her macaroni and forced herself to swallow. The macaroni was extremely gross; it was cold, hard, and had no cheese flavor at all. Reba swallowed and gulped her water down silently. Reba wiped her mouth with the back of her hand and looked at the rest of her friends.

Reba's eyes widened with horror as she saw Peyton take a spoonful of her macaroni and slowly bring it to her mouth. Reba bit her lip as Peyton chewed and listened to Kat talk about another prank call she had made when she was younger. Peyton's face scrunched up and looked down at the macaroni. Peyton swallowed and cried out, "Yuck!"

"What?" Abigail asked.

"Yuck! This is terrible! This macaroni! Who made this? Ewww!" Peyton called.

Everyone looked around the table, including Reba so she wouldn't look guilty.

"Reba made the yucky macaroni and cheese; I told you it was gross Reba! I should have warned you all not to eat it!" Abigail's father said.

Reba turned red and looked at Peyton, who was chugging her water.

"Well, we aren't all perfect," Erin defended Reba. Reba gave Erin a grateful look.

"It's okay Reba. It is hard to make macaroni that is any good anyways," Brooke comforted. Reba smiled at her too.

Abigail's father turned on his heel and left.

Peyton suddenly began talking about some random topic and left Kat's story in the dust bin of history.

Reba didn't even eat a bite of her food, she went home before Peyton had finished her story.

In the Way of the Juice:

✦

Collin

Collin had been very surprised three times in less than 24 hours. First, he discovered that Cole went to his preschool, second, Reba had visited him for some butter, and third, he had won a trip to Washington DC and a lifetime supply of sunscreen and lotion.

Collin was flipping through his preschool yearbook, looking for clues to the Cole mystery, when the doorbell rang.

"Collin could you get that? I'm in the shower!" Collin's mom yelled.

"Yes mom," Collin yelled back.

He opened the door in time to see a UPS truck driving away and a small package by his feet. It was addressed to him from Connie and Amelia Williams! The sweepstakes ladies! Collin excitedly grabbed the package and brought it inside.

He ripped off the paper and pulled out three items: a bottle of sunscreen, a tiny bottle of lotion, and a picture of the White House. On the back of the picture of the White House it said:

Dear Collin Fellers,

I hope you enjoy the lifetime supply of lotion and sunscreen we gave you. We hope you are a person who likes to tan, because if you are ,you may need more sunscreen. Here is a picture of Washington DC, please pretend you are there. Imagination is the only ticket you need.

   Sincerely,
   Connie Williams
   Amelia Williams
   Connie Williams and Amelia Williams

Collin's brow furrowed, he threw the 'prizes' back into the box and returned to his yearbook, with no success.

Monday morning came and Collin eagerly told his friends what he had found out.

"So Cole went to your preschool," Steve said. "That doesn't help us one bit."

"It's a start," Collin tried.

"Not a very good one," Mitch commented.

"Well why don't you go ask Cole again?" Collin suggested.

"Of course I am going to ask Cole again!" Mitch declared.

"Want to know something weird that happened to me this weekend?" Steve asked. "I got a call from an elderly lady telling me I had to go shave my face and go to war or else I would suffer. Isn't that crazy?"

"I'll tell you what is crazy; I got a call from a radio show host for an interview! It was nuts! She kept asking me random questions like what I plan to do in the next hour! It was the most bizarre thing ever!" Mitch exclaimed.

"I have an even more bizarre story than that!" Collin quickly recalled his telephone call and 'prizes'.

"That is so strange!" Steve commented.

"I'll say!" Mitch agreed.

The bell sent them all to class.

Collin did not leave his table at lunch. He didn't dare risk being tormented by Andy and Reese. He drank his tomato juice while Steve made 'constructive criticism' on Robert's lunch.

"Those cookies will not help you think at all! And a juice box is incredibly bad for your teeth! And is that bacon? Goodness gracious! Why on earth are you eating bacon?" Steve babbled on and on. Robert didn't seem to mind that Steve disapproved of his lunch.

Collin did think it was odd that Robert was eating bacon for lunch. Robert always ate unhealthy food, always. It would be a lie to say that Robert's weight was normal. Robert was definitely a little pudgy. Or a lot pudgy. But Collin didn't make friends because of how they looked. He made friends because of how they acted, and Robert was a kind fellow indeed.

Steve finished commenting on Robert's lunch after Robert offered him a cookie. Then Robert offered everyone else a delicious cookie. Collin liked the cookie very much and was about to ask Robert for another when Andy Koller grabbed Robert's cookies.

"Hey! We were eating those!" Steve defended.

"I'm hungry," was Andy's reply.

"Then go eat your lunch! Or go get a free bag of chips from the snack bar! You don't have to take our food!" Steve cried.

"Think of it as an act to end world hunger," Reese came up from behind Collin and Steve.

"How 's stealing an act of charity?" Steve asked.

"I'm hungry, thus contributing to world hunger. I am another hungry person! But now because of these lovely cookies, there is less world hunger!" Andy explained before stuffing the cookies into his mouth.

"Mmmm, what are these?" Reese asked, picking up Steve's pretzels.

"They aren't yours, they're mine! Now leave us alone!" Steve ordered.

"Why don't you share? C'mon! Don't be such a hog!" Andy whined.

Collin's head slowly spun around to look for Cole, but he didn't see Cole anywhere.

"Lookin' for Cole? He is in math," Andy informed, sticking his face in Collin's.

"Why is he in math? Detention?" Mitch asked, trying to sound casual.

"Why do you need to know, Stalker?" Reese hopped behind Mitch and grabbed Mitch's shoulders, causing Mitch to lurch forward.

"Reese! Here, take my sandwich and go away!" Mitch cried, thrusting a turkey sandwich at Reese.

Reese took the sandwich, stuffed it in his mouth, and swallowed nosily, keeping his grip on Mitch's shoulders.

"What? Why won't you leave?" Antonio asked.

"I am thirsty!" Reese declared.

"We aren't your servants! Go get a drink from the drinking fountain," Mitch said.

"No, I want a juice box!" Reese said in a whiny voice, imitating a toddler.

"Hey bro, looky here! Looks like our buddy Antonio has a juice box!" Andy snatched up Antonio's juice box and handed it to Reese.

"Thank you!" Reese took the juice box from Andy and threw his head back, opening his mouth widely. Then he positioned the juice box so that the slightest tip of the box would send a waterfall of juice into Reese's mouth. Reese tipped the box and pulled his head back, causing the juice to splash onto Mitch's head.

"Hey!" Collin cried. Even though the juice landed on Mitch, Collin knew the embarrassment Mitch felt.

"Whoops! Sorry dude! Guess next time you shouldn't have been in the way of the juice!" Reese sneered.

Steve opened his mouth and began protesting that Mitch had done nothing to deserve juice on his head. Mitch showed no signs of annoyance or hurt; he simply stood up and took off to the bathroom without making a sound or gesture.

"Jeez Steven, I didn't know you wanted juice on your head too," Andy said with fake surprise.

"I don't want juice on my head! I don't! Stop!" Steve commanded as Reese handed Andy the juice box.

Then Collin saw something amazing. It was a gigantic act of great bravery and loyalty. Collin felt almost embarrassed for not being brave enough to do the act of bravery Antonio did.

As Andy grabbed the juice box and pulled it toward him, Antonio's hand reached out and grabbed the box out of Andy's hand.

Every face at the table showed great shock, including Andy and Reese's.

"That is mine, thank you. I was planning to drink it, and if you waste it by spilling it all over my friends' heads, I won't be able to get a sip of juice," Antonio said promptly before sucking juice through the straw.

Enraged, Andy snatched the box from Antonio and squeezed it above Antonio's head. But to Collin's surprise, nothing came out. Andy was surprised too and tried again and again to make Antonio's head wet with juice. Antonio sat in his seat smiling, as if he had planned it (which he most likely had).

Andy smashed the juice box on Antonio's head and stomped off, fuming. Reese grabbed Collin's sandwich and followed Andy.

Collin didn't even care that his sandwich was gone; he was too busy marveling at Antonio. Steve clapped and Robert slapped Antonio on the back.

"Antonio! That was brilliant! Absolutely brilliant!" Collin congratulated his friend. Antonio's face couldn't have been brighter if it was the baby of a star and the sun.

Robert, Steve and Collin hadn't gotten close to finishing their praise for Antonio when Andy suddenly came at Antonio, running full speed. Before Antonio could even remove his smile, Andy had stuffed a cheese pizza in his face and pulled Antonio's shirt over Antonio's head, causing the pizza to stay put in its place over Antonio's eyes and nose.

Reese handed Andy a full juice box and Andy dumped it on Antonio's head while saying in a fake sweet voice "There you go; now you can have all the juice you want!"

Collin turned and saw that almost all the people in the lunchroom were watching, most of them were snickering silently. It was times like these that Collin wished the school's lunch attendant wouldn't sleep on the job.

Andy finished crushing the juice box on Antonio's head and ran the opposite way he had come, which meant Andy had to pass Collin's table. Collin knew this was his only chance to stick up for his friend, so when Andy ran by, Collin reached out his hand and grabbed Andy's belt loop.

It seemed to have happened in slow motion. Andy's feet flew in the air behind him, causing Andy to fall forward. He would have broken his nose if his arms hadn't been ready to break his head's fall to the concrete ground.

Andy was physically okay, no bruises or scratches of any sort, but Collin had not let go of Andy's belt loop. Andy's head was on the floor, but his pants weren't. Collin had held onto the pants, so they slid right down to Andy's knees when Andy fell. The entire cafeteria was a witness.

It took everyone, even Collin, a while to realize what had just happened. Collin was the first to realize it, and when he did he let go of Andy's belt loop, as if to cover up his vengeful action, and let the rest of Andy's body fall to the floor.

Andy was the second to realize what had happened and scrambled to pull his pants back over his boxer shorts. The rest of the cafeteria was the third to realize what had happened. No one laughed; two people started to snicker but stopped halfway.

Collin sat frozen in his seat. Thoughts and emotions mixed and fought to be the one that Collin would feel. Did Collin regret what he had just done? He wasn't sure. Collin definitely showed Andy that he was more than a punching bag, but now Collin was about to be beat black and blue by Andy Koller. Collin was paralyzed by fear. He watched as Andy emotionlessly, slowly stood up, brushed himself off, and walked away. Collin tried to read Andy's face for any sign of revenge or truce. But Andy's face was an erased whiteboard. There was nothing to read. Andy walked away with Reese trailing behind him.

Collin felt a twinge of giddiness. Maybe now that Andy had been stood up to twice, he would stop harassing Collin and his friends. Collin turned to face his audience. The entire cafeteria could be described in three words: shocked, amazed, dumfounded. Mouths hung open and whispers floated through the room.

Collin's ears opened up to receive the applause Collin knew he deserved. But the cafeteria stayed silent. People stood up and left, still whispering.

The silence shot through Collin's heart and sent his brain spinning with questions. With an attempt to heal Collin's heart by breaking the silence, the shrill bell screamed at the students. The cafeteria began to empty, and Collin turned to look at Steve, Robert, and Antonio. Antonio had gotten his shirt down and pulled the pizza off his face.

Steve's mouth was hanging open, but was angled upward into an awkward smile. Robert shook his look of disbelief off his face and replaced it with a smile. Antonio did the same.

"Collin! Thank you! Thank you! You sure showed him! We are escalating up the social list fast!" Antonio cheered as he wiped pizza sauce off his face and put his lunch in the trash.

"Well it is only a matter of time before Mitch, Robert and I commit a noble deed as well," Steve teased.

The friends quickly packed up, complimenting the heroes of the day generously.

"Oh, Mitch! He hasn't come back yet! I'll give him his stuff. His classroom is right next to mine," Collin said just as he was about to leave the table.

Collin gripped Mitch's backpack firmly in one hand and hurried to find his best friend.

Collin found Mitch standing behind a bench, smiling proudly.

"Andy lied! Andy lied!" Mitch sang when Collin approached him.

"What?" Collin was confused why Mitch wasn't praising him for his act of bravery.

"I peeked into Cole's math class, and it turns out that Cole wasn't in detention or anything bad at all! He was doing extra credit and getting a special advanced math lesson," Mitch said excitedly.

"Pardon?"

"The math lesson was optional. It wasn't going to be on a test, and the rest of the class wasn't going to learn it. It was only if you wanted to! He went into math for fun! And he was doing an extra credit paper that he asked for! I saw him walk up to the teacher and ask her for a math sheet that he could do in his free time! Collin, my hypothesis is correct! Cole is not another Andy clone; he is not a bad guy or a bully. Cole is what Andy would call a nerd or geek!" Mitch was so excited that he was actually hopping up and down.

"Wow, that is something to think about," Collin said as he shook his head.

"Yes!"

"Did you see what happened at lunch after you left?"

Mitch looked confused and was about to ask for details when the janitor shouted, "30 seconds to the bell!"

Collin bolted into his classroom without saying another word to Mitch.

"And then Andy stood up and walked away without a word!" Steve finished telling the complete tale of what happened in lunch to Mitch after school.

"Amazing! Good job Antonio! And Collin too!" Mitch smiled and shook Antonio's shoulder.

"This is a big, big statement! This is going to change so much!" Mitch cheered.

Collin did not feel the same way as his friends. His friends were exuberant about how Collin and Antonio had stuck up to Andy. They were especially pleased with Andy's exit. They assumed that it meant Andy would stop bullying them, but Collin saw it as a doorway to more extreme harassment. Collin worried for his friends because they were closing their eyes when they should be pinning them open. His friends were relaxing and taking their guard down when they should be making plans of defense.

But was that really what they should be doing? Planning defense? Or should they be making plans to attack? All this time they have been defending, not fighting. They ran from the problem and sat silently while the abuse piled on. They had tried to send the enemy in a different direction, hoping the enemy would just go away, but now was the first time they had actually fired their own bullets, used their own weapons. It looked like fighting back had stopped the enemy, but Collin thought it only built a bridge for Andy and Reese.

Collin never liked fighting. Fighting meant getting dirty and rumpling your shirt. Fighting was slob-like. And since Collin was not a slob, he never fought. Until now, of course. And maybe his friends were right, maybe the bullying would go away, only time could tell.

The Masked Friends:

Reba

Reba dreaded going to school that Monday, but she eventually ended up at school anyway. She didn't look at Collin when she went out to put her backpack in the car and saw he was doing the same. She couldn't look at almost anybody. She was too ashamed of the prank calls she had let happen before her very eyes.

But she had to eat lunch with her friends, so Reba walked over to her friends' table and sat down next to Peyton, who was yakking away, as usual. Reba's friends didn't mention the party at all, they simply listened, or pretend to listen, as Peyton babbled on and on about something completely stupid.

Reba chewed and swallowed her sandwich as she always did. Her lunches were always very much the same; Peyton talked, everyone else ate. Reba didn't mind it at all; in fact she was almost glad today that none of her friends beside Peyton had a chance to talk because it might open a window for a conversation about the party.

"And then I went on another roller coaster! This one went upside down…" Peyton chattered, when she was interrupted by a flushed and excited looking Kat, who had just come back to Reba's table from buying her lunch.

"Sorry Peyton, but you won't want to miss hearing this!" Kat apologized with a huge grin on her face. "Okay, so Andy and Reese were messing with that group of nerds that always sit by the door and that kid, uhm, Cohen right? The one with the blonde hair?"

"Collin," Reba offered.

"Yeah yeah, Collin. So anyway, Collin pantsed Andy! He totally pulled Andy's pants down!" Kat said excitedly.

Reba wasn't sure exactly how she felt about this. She was delighted that someone did something to stand up to Andy, but at the same time she wondered if giving Andy his own medicine was the way it should be done.

"Ewww, why would someone do that? What a party pooper! I bet it totally ruined the entire prank Andy was playing," Peyton said, disgusted.

"Yeah, I mean, it isn't going to win a dork anymore status or anything if he sticks up to his tormentor," Erin shook her head.

"But do you really think Collin should have let Andy embarrass Collin, or do whatever Andy was doing?" Reba said before she could stop herself.

All of Reba's friends turned and stared at Reba, appalled.

"Well, yah I think Collin should have let Andy do what he was doing. He is a nerd. Who cares what happens to nerds?" Peyton asked.

Reba nodded, struggling not to say that she cared and so should Peyton.

"So uhm, what happened at the roller coaster?" Reba asked timidly, trying to get the topic off Andy or nerds.

"Oh, the roller coaster did a whole bunch of zigzags," Peyton continued with her story as if nothing had happened.

Reba waited for her friends to stop staring at her before she started on her sandwich again. It took almost a whole five minutes for Kat to stop staring at Reba. When she finally did, Reba relaxed.

The next day at lunch, Reba prayed that nothing would come up that would make her have an outburst. Luckily, nothing happened until the very end of the lunch period, when Andy and Reese came over to Reba's table for the second time that year.

"Hi Andy," Peyton said smiling.

Andy nodded before telling the girls his news, "Remember when I told you Reese and I were planning to prank Collin? Well, we have thought of the best prank yet!"

Andy leaned in and said the rest in a very, very, very quiet whisper, "We are going to pants Collin, underwear and all. The little dork will be standing there with no bottoms on! Full moon! Bring a camera, we can take pictures and post them on the internet or something. It will be great revenge for what the dork did to me! And I know you won't tell anyone who would tell Collin."

"Oh, this is going to be the best! When will it take place?" Kat asked happily.

"Tomorrow, after school," Reese informed.

"How will you make sure Collin is there?" Abigail asked.

"I am going to give him this," Reese placed a scrap of paper on the table that read:

Collin, meet me after school on the lower field. Don't talk about it to my face or say anything about it to anyone else. I will explain it all when we get there- Mitch.

"Genius!" Peyton exclaimed.

"Get there early, and hide good!" Andy advised.

"Wait, what about your friend that sticks up for the nerds?" Erin asked.

"Cole? He has baseball practice directly after school, and we aren't going to tell him anyway, so you better not either!" Andy warned and left.

The last thing on earth Reba wanted to do was go to the lower field the next day after school. She began listing excuses in her mind for her not to go. By the time she arrived home, she had a couple good ones. The first one she would use would be that her mom needs her to be home immediately after school; the second one would be that she got detention. If you look in the dictionary, a couple means two. Reba only had a couple, or two, excuses for her not to watch Collin be pantsed after school.

While Reba was doing her homework, the phone rang. Reba's mom answered it. Afterward, Reba's mother informed Reba that Peyton had called to offer to take Reba home tomorrow.

"Did you say yes?" Reba asked, hoping the answer was no.

"Of course! I could use the extra time to get more done at work!" Reba's mother answered brightly.

Reba's stomach did a nervous dance. She hoped her friends would believe she had detention.

"I have detention, I am so disappointed! I can't believe I am going to miss this!" Reba whined to her friends the next day after school. She had walked up to them with a devastated expression and stomped her foot to get their attention and to show that she was angry. Reba hadn't really gotten a detention, of course.

"Did you get your detention today?" Brooke asked, her eyes were full of worry that her friend would miss getting to see Collin be humiliated.

"Yes," Reba replied.

"Oh, then you can go!" Kat exclaimed.

"Why?"

"Because detentions are for the day after you receive them. I know because I have gotten a few in my life," Kat explained.

"Oh, yippee!" Reba punched her fist in the air and did her best to look excited.

"Let's go quick! Before Collin gets there!" Abigail said. She pulled out her camera, prepared as usual, and took off to the field.

When Reba didn't go fast enough, Brooke pulled Reba along with her, causing Reba to jog. When they got to the field, Reba hid behind the bleachers with a few other people.

A lot of people showed up to witness the event. A lot of people. Reba wondered if Collin would spot them and leave. She hoped so very much.

"Shh!" someone hissed.

Everyone was silent, and Reba saw Collin coming down the ramp across the field. Reba saw that three or four jackets were lying on the bleachers and guessed that Collin thought they were Mitch. Collin took long strides to the bleachers, and Reba's stomach tightened with every one.

Collin was now close enough to see that the jackets were not Mitch and had stopped a few yards away from them. Collin turned around so that his back was facing his audience. Reba spotted Andy as he rose from his crouched position and quietly stepped in Collin's direction,.

Reba could barely believe this was going to happen. Her conscience screamed at her to do something, but her body refused.

Suddenly Reba had a flash back; she and Collin were in Collin's playroom nine years ago. Collin and Reba were building a tower with blocks. It was as tall as them, but Collin's dog knocked it over with its bushy tail. Collin and Reba had laughed. They didn't care that the tower was knocked down. They were just happy to be playing together.

Reba suddenly returned to the present. Collin didn't deserve this at all. All Collin did was be himself. Something most people can't do. Most people would go past the limit of not being themselves to fit in and be accepted. There are very few people who would be themselves without a second thought. Collin was one of those people. Collin was brave for following his heart and not changing to please someone else. He didn't change even though he was bullied for being who he was.

All the people sitting around Reba were wearing masks, and underneath the mask, if you looked very hard, you might find who those people really are.

Collin never wore a mask once in his life.

And now he was going to be punished for it. But why? People classified as nerds and dorks can't help being who they are. They can't help if they need glasses or braces or were born with some kind of mental problem. And even if they came to school one day in the most expensive car and coolest clothes, they would be bullied even more. There is nothing they can do to escape the bullying. To escape who they are.

Reba was not going to let Collin be punished for being himself.

Andy was less than a foot away from Collin and had his hands ready to pull down Collin's pants.

Reba stepped out of her hiding spot, and yelled as loud as she could, "Collin! Run!"

Climbing Out:

Collin

Collin turned and saw Andy inches away from him with his hands behind Collin's waist. Collin ran. No, he didn't just run, he sprinted. He sprinted up the ramp and across the blacktop. He saw Andy begin to run after him, but Collin had a huge head start because Andy was so surprised at what had happened. Collin knew where he was going; he was going to the office.

Collin also knew who had yelled. Reba.

Collin burst into the office. Papers flew out of the hands of the surprised secretary.

"Andy Koller is chasing me! He is going to get me! I am sorry about the papers, but you must help me!" Collin begged.

The secretary took ten seconds to realize what was happening and called the principal. The principal, appeared at Collin's side and listened to Collin's story until Andy Koller stopped outside the office.

Andy must have seen the principal, because Andy began walking back the way he had come.

"Not so fast, young man!" The principal stepped out of the office and grabbed Andy's shoulder.

Collin smiled because he knew he had just climbed out of the hole he fell in so many years ago.

Part I of Epilogue:

Reba

You may be wondering what happened to Reba after she yelled to Collin, well here is exactly what happened:

Andy and all of Collin's audience turned and stared at Reba. But this time she felt no shame in what she had done. She stood tall and proud.

When Andy took off running after Collin, people began shouting at Reba. Reba did not back down or lose her pride.

"Why did you do that?"

"What was that for?"

"What is your problem?" These were all thrown at Reba.

But no one came out of their hiding place. They all stayed put.

"I'll tell you why," Reba replied confidently.

"Because why did Collin deserve this? What did Collin do to deserve any of his torture?" Reba asked the crowd.

"He is a dork!" Reese called.

"He pantsed Andy!" someone else offered.

"Why did he stand up to Andy? Because Andy was tormenting him! Collin has been bullied and tortured every day of his life. And why? Why does he or any of his friends deserve to be bullied the way they are? Why do they deserve to be laughed at and be given no sympathy? Why is their every move mocked and made fun of?" Reba preached.

"Because they are dorks! They don't have feelings!" Someone shouted.

"Of course they have feelings, you idiot! Everyone has feelings!" Reba shot back. "What are they supposed to do about being a 'dork'? They can't do anything! Would you still make fun of them if they got contacts? If they got their braces off? Of course you would still make fun of them. There is nothing they can do to change who they are. There is nothing they can do to stop the teasing. Once they are labeled as dorks, they stay a dork."

No one said a word.

"And it's not just 'dorks'! People can't help if they have a bad acne problem or a big nose! You people criticize others for things they can't help! You should practice what you preach!" Reba said.

Confused expressions sprinkled the faces of the audience.

"How many of you have said 'follow your heart' or 'be yourself'? Collin and his friends have done that! They don't spend the day hiding under make up, or acting like they like something they don't. They wear what they want and act how they are. They are themselves! And yet, you punish them for it!" Reba cried.

"Next time you are about to criticize someone, please, please ask yourself why. They probably have enough on their plate as it is! Imagine how hard their everyday life must be!" Reba finished. She felt the best she had ever felt in her entire life.

"Bogus!" Reese walked off muttering to himself. No one else did or said anything.

Reba turned and walked away. She decided to let her words sink in.

Part II of Epilogue:

Collin

So much happened after the day Collin arrived on the lower field and ran. Reese and Andy were expelled. Reba's little speech got all around the school, even to the teachers.

People, who Collin didn't even know would come up to him and apologize for being a jerk and talking about him behind his back. But they didn't just apologize to Collin; they also apologized to Steve, Antonio, Mitch, and Robert.

On Saturday evening, Reba knocked on Collin's front door. Collin answered it and saw Reba in tears. She threw her arms around Collin and apologized over and over for not being his friend the last couple years and allowing so many bad things to happen to him.

"Oh, oh Collin! I am so sorry!" Reba cried.

"It's okay," Collin stated. He said it as a statement, not as a comfort.

Reba had looked at him with big red eyes and smiled. Then she laughed and asked how things could have gotten so messed up.

Another loose end was still not tied up, and Collin was not going to let himself wonder anymore. What was Cole's secret?

At lunch, Collin marched straight up to Cole and demanded to know what was going on.

"Huh?" Cole asked.

"Mitch asked you what you meant when you said 'I'm not going there again' and you told him your full name and to not tell me. Later I discovered you in my preschool yearbook," Collin explained quickly.

"I can't believe you don't remember. Collin, do you remember The Mean Boy?" Cole asked.

Of course Collin remembered. The Mean Boy pushed Collin down and stole his lunch in preschool. He had stepped on Collin's toes and cut him in line. The Mean Boy had tormented Collin from preschool to second grade. In the middle of second grade The Mean Boy had moved away.

"That was you?" Collin asked.

Cole nodded.

"I feel so bad about how I acted when I was little; I needed to make it up to you. But I didn't want you to realize it was me from preschool and spread a reputation of me as being a jerk. I've changed a lot since then, and I'm really sorry, Collin. I really am," Cole apologized.

"I have heard more people say sorry to me than you would believe. Cole, I forgive you. Let's start over," Collin reached out his hand to Cole.

Cole took it and smiled. The two boys walked back to Collin's lunch table, where Reba sat also.

Part III of Epilogue:

Reba

Yes, you did read right, Reba was sitting at Collin's table at lunch. In fact, she had sat there every day since her speech. Reba did not want to be friends with people without hearts, so she sat with the truest and kindest person she knew: Collin.

To Reba's surprise, other people began sitting with Collin and his friends also. Reba got to know all of Collin's friends really well, and they were great people too. Sure they weren't perfect, but who is? Collin's group grew and grew; people started describing it as a welcoming place and the place to go when you feel bad.

No one was told they weren't allowed to sit with Collin and his friends. Reba was surprised to see Brooke eating lunch next to Antonio one day and chatting with him.

"Brooke! What are you doing here?" Reba asked.

"Reba, your speech said a lot to me. I never realized how cruel I was being. You are a true role model Reba. I really wish I could be more like you," Brooke said.

"I'm glad Brooke. I really am," Reba said.

All kinds of people sat in the group. People called weirdoes and freaks. People you would shy away from or laugh at and point at sat at the group. Reba got to know all of them, and they were all great.

Reba made tons of friends, and self confidence was won by many students. Respect was given to the weirdoes. The students in the school looked with new eyes and saw what really mattered, not what people looked like.

No one was teased. Friends were made. The entire school, and I mean every person, was changed. People began coming to school without worrying if they would be criticized or not.

No one was wearing a mask anymore.

Collin and Reba became better friends than when they were babies. They spent every weekend doing something together, whether it was going to the park or homework.

"Reba, please come up for your show-and-tell," Mr. Lavalonski said.

It was show-and-tell week. A month earlier, Reba would probably have tried to learn some amazing talent or have bought a lizard so that she would have something interesting to show.

But a month earlier, Reba was very different.

Reba walked up to the front of the classroom and smiled, "Ladies and gentlemen, for my show-and-tell I am going to show you something about me."

Reba pulled out her hearing aid.

"I am part deaf in one ear and whole deaf in the other. I wear this hearing aid all the time," Reba announced proudly.

No one said anything hurtful to Reba. No one ever would.